THE CELLAR AT NO. 5

Mrs. Rampage lives alone, in a large house cluttered with her precious objets d'art. Her daughter is half a world away, and her niece has no time for the old lady. So Mrs. Rampage is persuaded — much against her will — to take a companion into her home: Mrs. Roach, a poor but respectable widow. As resentment mounts between the pair, a violent confrontation is inevitable when the suppressed tension finally boils over . . .

SHELLEY SMITH

◆

THE CELLAR
AT NO. 5

Complete and Unabridged

LINFORD
Leicester

First published in Great Britain in 1954

First Linford Edition
published 2017

A catalogue record for this book is available
from the British Library.

ISBN 978–1–4448–3457–4

1

As soon as the letters flopped on the mat, down she stumped in her broken mules to get them, the trailing wrap exposing her thin legs in their wrinkled stockings, the strings of her sleeping cap dangling. Before she even reached the mat, Mrs. Rampage could see that the letter she wanted was not there. Poor old dear, nothing but buff envelopes! She leafed through them . . . bills . . . bills . . . bills . . . or receipts. No, nothing from Jonquil.

It was more than merely a sickening disappointment; anxiety turned like a familiar key in the lock of her heart. Not hearing always gave her the horrible lurching sensation that some disaster must have occurred — though she ought to have been familiar with her daughter's lethargy as a correspondent.

And here it was, her birthday, and not so much as a pretty card from anyone else to make her feel not quite so hopelessly neglected.

'Poor old Mum!' she said aloud, derisively. 'No one remembers her now!'

With the post in her hand, she opened the door on her left and went stumbling across the black room, banging into the furniture, to undo the heavy iron bars that fastened the shutters and let in the frosty morning light.

It was going to be a fine day; and cheered by this omen she at once decided that there would be a letter from her by the second post. Jonquil would never have forgotten her birthday, that was out of the question. *It was out of the question*, she told herself sharply, so what was she fussing about so absurdly?

She stood in the middle of the elegant drawing room — dishevelled, gross old body balanced on spindly legs — scanning her mail, a grotesque figure among the Sheraton, the ormolu and marquetry, the gilt and brocade. Yet the light — pouring down through tall Georgian windows to run brilliant white fingers down her satin wrap, to find a diamond of light in the corner of her eye, to glint on a fingernail, to discover silver and porcelain against the dark panelled walls — turned the little scene from something ludicrous into a glowing little interior of the Dutch school; say, a Gerard Terborch.

Then she crammed the bills impatiently back into their envelopes, and the light broke up and slipped away like quicksilver.

Off she stumped to the basement to get her breakfast. A basement kitchen in this day and age! There was indeed a wild incongruity about the clinical whiteness of stove and refrigerator in that stone-flagged old dungeon.

Mrs. Rampage stood by the kitchen table, spooning up her cereal hurriedly because she disliked it and wanted to get rid of it as quickly as possible, yet could never be bothered to make herself anything nicer.

'Delicious!' she declared as she finished, and even smacked her lips.

When the kettle boiled she made a cup of coffee substitute, gulped it down, and then rinsed the bowl and the cup under the tap and left them to dry on the draining board. That was breakfast done.

To see her, one would imagine there was not a moment to spare; instead of nothing to do and all day to do it in. Mrs. Rampage never got dressed until she had done the housework. She liked to slop about comfortably in her corsets and an old satin wrap. Three mornings a week a woman came in to do the rough for her — 'A positive angel, a treasure,' Mrs. Rampage called her, but still, she could not be expected to do everything; moreover, Mrs. Rampage liked to look after the old period stuff herself. No one else could be trusted. Besides, she enjoyed washing her pieces of Dresden, or using one of her cherished recipes for cleaning old ivory or bringing up the colour of faded wood. With her daughter so far away, there was little else to her life now; her one great interest was in her collections. Time passed most happily for her when she was turning over the rubbish in some seedy old junk shop.

No. 5 was a tall old house, of which only one eye (the landing window) was visible to the road behind the high brick wall. Mrs. Rampage lived there alone, now that she was alone. It was certainly an inconvenient house and much too large for her ('All those stairs!' complained her friends), but she could not be brought to give it up; she loved it. She was enormously proud of it; its panelled rooms, the long twisting staircase with the barley-sugar balustrade, the beautiful Adam architraves, all filled her with delight. Also, she had been obliged to spend a great deal of money on doing it up and keeping it in repair (dilapidated gutters, ancient plumbing, rotting joists could run up a pretty penny), and what costs one dear is inevitably dear to one, it is a logic of human nature. Yet it was not only her pride in it, not only that she had spent more money on it than she could hope to get back, it was something more painful than that, something to do with Jonquil — though Jonquil had never seen it. It was the intimation that if she gave it up and went to live elsewhere there would be a whole epoch of her life that Jonquil would never be able to place, the entire events of a chapter lost forever to her. And each tiny additional separation, physical or mental, was freshly distressing to Mrs. Rampage, was a hideous little death.

Everyone was agreed that, if there was a subject on which witty Mrs. Rampage could become a bore, it was that tiresome girl. How she went on about her! With the excited adoring expression of a lover, which made it more irritating still. But then no one understood that Jonquil was her religion; a religion devoted to the depths of possessiveness, of self-love, of daughter worship. As mystics can contemplate for unmeasured periods images and abstractions of the Only and the All, so Mrs. Rampage could meditate on her recollections of Jonquil. With one part of her mind she was thinking of her now, while she slid the mop across the floor.

After four years it was difficult to fancy what Jonquil was like or what life she led, and she was obliged to muddle images of her as she remembered her against imagined backgrounds. Strangely enough, no ghostly image of the man Jonquil had married haunted these meditative exercises of hers — she put the thought of him from her mind.

The parquet looked so splendid, quite like Mrs. Mouse's in the advertisement, that in another compartment of her mind she decided to give the daily woman her old red cardigan that had the moth. But when she found a thick, disgusting nest of cobwebs behind the grandfather clock, she changed her mind.

'Filthy slut!' she cried angrily, slashing at them with her duster. They were all the same, every one of them! 'Presumably it requires too much effort to look behind or underneath a piece of furniture,' she scolded Lily Graveyard in her mind. 'Half-a-crown an hour for a little dainty dusting, plus elevenses and a nice chat sitting on your great fat bottom, and you call that a morning's work!'

Not quite fair to Miss Graveyard, a small driven woman who slaved away as if Mrs. Rampage had set a devil at her heels.

The telephone startled her, and she ran to tackle it as if it were an exploding geyser. She always handled it gingerly and bawled into it loud enough to crack your eardrums if you were on the receiving end.

This was a friend of hers ringing to wish her many happy returns.

'My dear, don't remind me!' implored Mrs. Rampage. 'At my age one tries to forget. Ha, ha!' With her free hand she rubbed the duster over the gilt Venetian mirror behind the phone while she listened to Geraldine's chatter. Her pallid reflection stuck out its tongue, and she leaned forward to examine it as seriously as a surgeon. Geraldine was being singularly boring, prosing on about her hypochondriac cousin's visit. As if anyone cared! And she was not apparently intending to invite her out, so Mrs. Rampage suddenly cried, 'My dear, I must fly, the milk's boiling over!' and hung up.

'Is that you, Lily?' she called over the banisters, hearing a noise below, but answer came there none. Bored, discouraged, she trailed her duster about. There ought to be something special about one's birthday, however old one was. If no one else was going to provide a treat for her, she'd give one to herself.

'I'll take you out, you old pet,' she said. 'We'll go and see if Etta's got anything interesting and you shall spend up to three pounds,' she promised, to cheer herself up.

Henrietta Purvis was her closest friend, her crony; and nothing — neither husbands, nor absence, not even Jonquil — had ever come between them. It was startling to them both to remember that they had been friends — yes! — for over fifty years. Funny little bosom pals toddling along to school in scarlet tammies and black woollen stockings — it made her laugh now to picture them — confiding giggling secrets to one another, or quarrelling tearfully. There was no one else in the world who knew as much about them as they knew about each other.

Henrietta, that rowdy good-hearted girl, had gone on the stage. But that was long ago; long, long ago. Enough had happened to her since then to fill a book. Her latest enterprise was an antique shop in Church Street, Kensington. She always declared she was doing very nicely, when Mrs. Rampage inquired, and the suspicion that she might be telling the truth was maddening to Mrs. Rampage, who considered that she knew far more about antiques than Henrietta. The point of her anxiety was that she might have been in on it too, if only she had had the pluck. For right at the beginning Henrietta had invited her to come in as a partner and put a thousand pounds into the business. She had refused because she was afraid of trusting her precious capital to Etta's plunging ignorance. Henrietta simply did not realize how painfully one could be stung.

''A little learning is a dang'rous thing; Drink deep, or taste not the Pierian spring',' Mrs. Rampage was fond of quoting. Privately, she was of the opinion that Henrietta ought to have been only too glad to take her as a partner for the value of her knowledge alone without expecting her to risk her money too, but Etta really did believe that she knew as much as Mrs. Rampage and even more.

Of course, there would have been the most dreadful quarrels if they had been in the business together, but Mrs. Rampage could not help thinking regretfully of the fun they would have had. Etta was a great old sport. Naturally, she *hoped* Henrietta would make a colossal success of it. But all the same, it would be very gratifying if she were to fail, despite Mrs. Rampage's good wishes.

The house bell chimed its two lucid notes.

'Why, it's Billy the postman!' she cried, counting him quite a friend of hers.

He thrust a parcel at her.

'A present! How lovely!' she cried ecstatically. As if it was a gift from the postman himself. Then, seeing it was not after all from Jonquil, called after him anxiously, 'Is that all for me?'

'That's all terday!' bawled the postman callously, banging the gate.

He was no friend but an enemy.

'Nothing to cry about, you silly old fool,' said Mrs. Rampage, coming in with the parcel in her arms and bumping the front door shut with her behind. 'She has probably missed the mail,' explained Mrs. Rampage, wiping her cheeks on the sleeve

11

of her wrap (but her stupid eyes kept filling with tears again).

'Well, fancy Rhoda remembering me!' she cried, trying to be pleased (Rhoda was her elder sister). 'Let's see what she's sent . . . Now, where did I put those scissors?' she asked, wandering upstairs. 'Scissors . . . ' she cried, tugging at the string, helplessly, a few angry, self-pitying tears slipping out again (she hated it in advance, whatever it was, because it was not from Jonquil and because there was nothing from Jonquil).

Unwrapped, the present was a capacious stuff workbag gathered onto a wooden frame, large enough to contain the *Queen Mary* and ugly enough to shake the foundation of the earth.

There was a note pinned to it in Rhoda's familiar wild scrawl. Mrs. Rampage put on her pink-rimmed spectacles and read:

I hope this will be useful to you — if you can still find time to do your lovely needlework.

Yr. affect. Sis,
Rhoda

This harmless little note made Mrs. Rampage practically gibber. She saw an insult in every word. Must have been quite a work of art to pack so many gibes into so small a compass. Rhoda could not really suppose it would be useful to her, she was always sending her these hideous workbags, what on earth could she imagine she did with them? Besides, Rhoda must remember perfectly well that she always used her beautiful Sheraton workbox for her needlework. And then that sneer about her finding *time*, meaning that only someone like Mrs. Rampage, with no family or responsibilities and no one but herself to consider, could possibly enjoy the leisure for such refinements nowadays. The allusion to her 'lovely needlework' was pure sarcasm, of course; Rhoda had always been jealous of her exquisite work.

Mrs. Rampage turned the bag inside out and angrily scrutinized the lining and stitches, like an ape searching for fleas; she was trying to think of some use she could put it to that would subtly avenge her for the imagined insult. She began to improvise a letter in her head.

'Dearest Rhoda,' she would say, 'how sweet of you to send me yet *another* lovely workbag for my birthday. The one you sent me for Christmas has been so useful, I really don't know what I should do without them all. One really can't have too many . . .'

Yet she was deeply fond of Rhoda, the last of the family. She had always admired her, always been a little afraid of her, sometimes had hated her (there had once been a quarrel lasting three years), and still, though Rhoda was seventy, could feel bitterly jealous of her. Jealous that Rhoda had a husband to look after and love her; it was unfair that they should live so contentedly up there in Cumberland on the farm Tom had bought after his retirement. Rhoda had simply no idea, sheltered by her husband, of what life was like for an elderly widow; the dreary loneliness of it with not much money and one's only child four thousand miles away. Rhoda scarcely ever came up to London now, and Mrs. Rampage really couldn't find the time to go all the way to

Cumberland on a visit just because Rhoda asked her. The sisters had not met for two years, and their lives had grown so far apart that they scarcely bothered to write to each other anymore; there seemed nothing to say. Just a little signal across the green fields of England at birthdays and Christmases to keep the blood of family feeling flowing.

The workbag was made of a good piece of stuff that could be used to make her a really serviceable pair of knickers for the winter. The suggestion of obscenity in this notion gratified Mrs. Rampage's desire for revenge. She felt quite cheerful again when she went down to have a chat with the daily woman.

She was in the mood for a gay little gossip. But Miss Graveyard was doleful. She sank back on her heels and gazed up at Mrs. Rampage with eyes like prunes in her small yellow face.

'My sister was took bad again yestiddy, maddam,' she began. It was a favourite opening.

'Oh, I am sorry.'

'Yes. Up half the night, I was, with her.

Oh, it was shocking to see her! I thought she'd go this time for sure.'

This kind of talk always made Mrs. Rampage want to giggle. She was simply no use at morbid conversation. She had no heart. To bite off her laughter, she said quickly:

'You poor thing! I expect you're feeling quite washed out. I was just going to make you a nice cup of tea. That'll buck you up.'

'Well, I won't say I couldn't use it, maddam,' Miss Graveyard said suitably.

But a moment later, Mrs. Rampage shrieked out from the kitchen: 'Lily, you *fiend*!'

'Now, maddam, what have I done?' cried poor Lily, running in with a white face.

'You've left the light on in the cellar, you bad girl!'

'I was just about to slip down there again with the shovel, maddam.'

'Well, you could have turned it on again,' Mrs. Rampage pointed out, quite pleasantly, and then she remembered something else: 'That reminds me; I don't know when you last cleaned the hall, but you can't have done behind the clock for months, it's too disgusting.'

In the low voice of a child answering her teacher, Miss Graveyard said: 'I do behind there every week, maddam.'

'Come and see for yourself,' Mrs. Rampage said, with a shrug.

Miss Graveyard stared at the evidence sullenly.

Always a fuss about something. Couldn't she as well have turned off the light herself and brushed away the cobweb? Oh, no, there always had to be a proper recitation about it; always showing off about something, maddam was. She got proper fed up with it, and that was a fact.

'If my work isn't satisfactory . . . ' said Miss Graveyard in a trembling voice.

'Now, Lily, I never said that. Don't be silly.'

'You can't expect to have this house kep' as it should be, for only three mornings a week; no one couldn't do it.'

'I'm not complaining. I know you're having a very worrying time and I make allowances.'

'On from morning to night,' said Miss Graveyard to the floor. 'It's more than flesh and blood can bear.'

'Lily, for goodness' sake don't upset yourself.'

'No, I'd rather give in my notice now and be done with it, if you please, maddam,' Miss Graveyard said, as if she were choking.

'Silly girl, don't I tell all my friends what a wonderful worker you are? Besides, it's my birthday today; I couldn't possibly accept your notice on my birthday,' Mrs. Rampage said gaily. 'I was going to give you that nice red cardigan of mine. It ought to just fit you now it's shrunk a little.'

Miss Graveyard blew her nose and sighed.

'Well, thank you, maddam, ever so,' Miss Graveyard said properly. And, having seen the moth holes, added: 'I dare say it will come in useful for something.'

She had given Mrs. Rampage quite a scare.

Mrs. Rampage went upstairs to dress. She put on the old mustard tweed skirt that she wore every day, and tugged a moss-green blouse over her bust. She leaned toward the glass and carelessly painted on some lips and eyebrows and two dabs of pink for the cheeks, and then dashed a flurry of powder over it to conceal the bruise on her cheek that ran up under one eye like a birthmark.

She was just frizzing her curls out over her forehead when Miss Graveyard put her all in a dither by yelling up that a Mrs. Getaway was downstairs. Cissie Getaway was her niece, and a visit from her at this hour of the morning was not only unexpected, it was unlikely; for even in these days Cissie could still pass for a richish woman, who had two proper maids and never rose before ten-thirty. Mrs. Rampage at once jumped to the conclusion that she brought bad news.

'Hallo, darling!' Cissie cried.

'Cissie, how nice to see you!' exclaimed Mrs. Rampage, adroitly pecking her magnolia cheek. 'Nothing wrong, I hope, dear?'

'Of course not, Auntie. Why should there be?'

Mrs. Rampage pushed the chairs about

nervously, wondering what it could be that Cissie wanted, then.

'You're looking marvellous,' she said insincerely, for she was too bothered even to glance at her. 'Come and sit by me and tell me what brings you to see your old aunt.'

'Your birthday, of course, Auntie.' She rummaged around in her handsome crocodile bag and brought out a small wrapped box.

'*No!* I'd forgotten all about it,' Mrs. Rampage declared. 'Do you mean to say you've come all this way just to see me?'

'Well, of course. Don't I always? I've brought you a little pressie.'

'Oh, Cissie darling, how naughty! What is it?'

'Open it and see,' suggested Mrs. Getaway.

'At my age one ought to forget the passing years,' Mrs. Rampage pretended, her short clumsy fingers tearing at the paper wrapping.

'I think that it's as one grows older that one needs a little something to cheer one up.'

Aunt Luna didn't even know how to acknowledge the present, just stared at it dumbly, the funny old thing.

'Well, do you like it, darling?'

'Much too good, much too good,' she said, and hastily put it down. It was a beautiful tooled leather box containing a set of seven seals in semi-precious stones, and Mrs. Rampage's reaction to it was one of suspicion. So valuable a gift was not for nothing. What did Cissie want?

But after a quarter of an hour, Cissie still had not come to the point of her visit, and was chatting away cheerfully about Cousin Emily's mad chauffeur and a ball she and Wilfred had been to at The Dorchester; and Mrs. Rampage chafed to see that the little gilt clock on the chimney piece already marked twenty past twelve; the morning gone . . . wasted; and she had meant to spend it rummaging happily in the back of Etta's shop, going through piles of Regency cartoons and hand-coloured prints from *La Belle Assemblée*.

And then it transpired that Cissie had taken tickets for the new Yvonne Arnaud comedy and was taking her out to lunch first. Then something must be very seriously wrong indeed, Mrs. Rampage decided; probably something to do with Wilfred. He was weak — weak, she had said so from the first. She could never trust a man with a mouth like that. Poor Cissie, with her unfortunate figure! Everyone knew he had married her for her money, and now he obviously resented it. Much easier to have a good talk about it all in the privacy of the home.

'Why eat out, dear? Such a waste of money, when I can open a tin and whip up something delicious in a minute!'

'Oh, no, Aunt Lu!' Cissie said quickly.

'It's not a bit of trouble.'

'The fact is, I'm on a very strict diet just now,' explained Cissie, who was terrified of her aunt's cooking.

'Why, I can do you a mousse as light as air in ten minutes, it couldn't hurt a baby. I just whip up some powdered milk in gelatine and beat in a tin of salmon and a spot of salad cream. It tastes just like The Ritz.'

'Darling, I'm absolutely forbidden to

eat anything tinned, it's poison to me.'

'Dear, if I may just give you a word of advice: men do hate women to be faddy over food.' (She had got it into her head that there was trouble between Cissie and Wilfred.)

'It's no treat for you to eat at home,' Cissie said firmly, and got her own way because she was accustomed to. One did not serve on committees for twenty years without developing an invincible technique for dealing with obstructive people and getting one's own way. Perhaps it was that peculiar ability that made one wish to serve on committees in the first instance, feeling the *power* of oneself as a social servant, organizing hospital welfare and clubs, and 'running' boroughs and councils. Cornered by Mrs. Getaway's massive bust, the most adamant adversaries caved in.

They lunched at Mrs. Getaway's club, in the handsome white dining room with the watered-silk panels and crystal chandeliers.

'Well, Nelly, how's Arthur getting on?' Mrs. Getaway asked the waitress pleasantly as she ordered.

Her practical benevolence extended to all the people who served her; she knew and remembered all the names and illnesses of their families. She was not an easy person to catch with a made-up tragedy. She could tell a liar's mouth, she could sum up character in the folding of a hand.

What was the latest news of Jonquil? she asked of Mrs. Rampage, eating her soup.

This was just what Mrs. Rampage enjoyed, and she went raving off boastfully, adding impossible embellishments of her own. Jonquil, with her gold and white beauty; Jonquil, about whom a maharajah had lost his head; Jonquil, who had been personally praised by the Governor for her work during the last cholera epidemic . . . But, alas, all this was old stuff that Cissie had heard the last time she saw Aunt Luna — more than a month ago.

'She ought to write to you more often,' the niece said pityingly.

'Oh, my dear, you don't know how busy she is. And she's so popular. Why, when the Earl of Lavenham stopped there on his way to Rangoon — '

'I know. But she only has one mother. She could make an effort to write more often.'

'Oh, she writes me the most wonderful letters,' Mrs. Rampage said loyally. 'Her descriptions! She should write a book.'

But Cissie was bored with that selfish girl. She said sharply: 'Aunt Lu, what's that bruise on your face?'

At No. 5 and in Cissie's Daimler, Mrs. Rampage had been able to keep that side of her face turned from her; but here, in the vast white dining room with its long windows filled with the bright October day, she could no longer hide it.

'This? Oh, nothing. It's nearly gone.'

'How did you do it?'

'Tell me about Wilfred,' Mrs. Rampage said hurriedly. 'They say he's so wonderfully clever at his job. Is it true?'

But Cissie was not to be sidetracked by Aunt Luna's innocent malice. 'What happened?' she said again.

'I was coming downstairs with a tray and I slipped, that's all. I thought I'd killed myself,' she laughed.

'Auntie, you really ought to be more careful! One of these days you'll hurt yourself and there'll be no one there to pick you up. I hope you had the doctor, anyway.'

'For a bruised bottom!' Aunt Luna said vulgarly. 'Whatever next? I simply popped into bed and lived on orange juice till I felt better. It would cost twenty pounds to have a cure like that in a sanatorium. And all it cost me was three and sixpence.'

'It wasn't sensible not to call in the doctor, Auntie, you might have injured yourself internally with a fall like that. You ought not to live alone, you know.'

'I really can't keep someone standing at the foot of the stairs all day in case I fall.' Mrs. Rampage giggled.

'No, I'm serious, Aunt Lu.'

For Mrs. Getaway did not like old ladies to live alone; she had seen so much of the misery, the tragedy, of old age, particularly lonely old age. One could hardly put it so bluntly to Aunt Luna, the poor old dear. Old ladies require tactful handling. And Aunt Luna was notoriously difficult, evasive, contrary, and inclined to cry poverty. Still, Mrs. Getaway chivvied at the subject as she had many times before; only each failure to persuade made the next attempt more pressing.

'It isn't fair to Jonquil, the other side of the world,' Cissie said cunningly.

'Heavens!' Mrs. Rampage said impatiently. 'You talk as if I was an old woman.'

'Darling, aren't you lonely?' Cissie pleaded. 'I should be frightened, living alone in that big house.'

But Mrs. Rampage never had time to be lonely, and as for being frightened, when she locked the shutters and barred the door what was there to be afraid of? It was no good Cissie arguing (and spoiling this delicious meal), she simply could not endure the notion of sharing her lovely house with anyone, lady or not. Someone else using her bathroom, and perhaps wanting to cook at odd hours, and then leaving the stove filthy, a mass of grease; oh, no thank you!

(For having gone through the argument that Mrs. Rampage could not possibly afford a servant to live in on her income, Cissie had ventured to suggest she might get a paying guest, or at least a lady to share the expenses of the house with her. But for all these suggestions Mrs. Rampage had an answer. They would not do, they would not do. P.G.s were always asking for glasses of hot water and leaving their dirty hairbrushes in the bathroom; lady sharers were sure to turn out either wildly extravagant or the kind that would scrutinize and argue over every item; and all servants were filthy sluts nowadays and absolute bitches to their employers, everyone knew; and anyway it would cost more than half her income to keep one — leaving practically nothing for Rates, Light, Telephone, Gardener, not to mention Food, Entertaining, Amusements or Holidays, she ended triumphantly, ticking off the items of this familiar litany on her short fingers.)

'I don't see why Jonquil shouldn't help toward it. Her husband sounds quite well-to-do,' Cissie said, hoisting Mrs. Rampage with her own petard, for she had bragged often enough of Guy Bracebridge's wealth.

'She would, if I'd let her,' Mrs. Rampage said quickly and untruthfully, and to change the subject took out of her bag the box of seals and began to examine them. She had not properly looked at them before. Now she saw that they were fashioned of beryl, and amethyst, and white topaz; and each bore, beside the day of the week, an inscription like *Amor nel Cor* or *Candor et Felix*, and a pretty little engraving of a Cupid or a dragon or a ship. She held each one to the light, enchanted.

'How could you bear to part with them, Cissie?' she now remarked. 'They're adorable! I've never noticed them before.'

'How should you? I've only just bought them.'

'You bought them!' Aunt Luna screeched like a cockatoo. (Cissie looked round quickly at the other diners.) 'You mean, you *bought* them? Are you mad? What did you want to do a thing like that for? Spending all that money! I know what they must have cost, don't tell *me*!'

'Really, Aunt Lu!' Cissie laughed. 'I'm only so pleased you like them.'

'No, I'm very angry with you. I mean it. There was no need to spend all that money; you've got plenty of little odds and ends at home that would have done for me.'

'Don't be so ungracious, darling.'

'Such a beastly little scarf I gave you for your birthday,' she moaned. 'But I'd just had that new hot-water tank put in, and I simply couldn't afford anything better.'

'Dear Aunt Lu, you're awfully clever over most things but sometimes you're an ass. Why must you judge everything by its price? There is a value that has nothing to do with money, you know.'

'Of course there is, darling; that's exactly what I'm saying. Wait till I show them to Henrietta; she'll go plaid with envy,' Mrs. Rampage assured her delightedly, reconciled by this thought to the value of the gift she had first been inclined to resent.

2

Cissie Getaway, glancing at the Empire mirror above the Queen Anne bureau at which she sat writing, saw its silvery surface darkened first by Edith's mulberry uniform and then filled with another dark shape. Edith mumbled something inaudible to the room at large and retreated. (She must speak to Edith again about announcing people properly.) The glass hung where it was so that she could observe unobserved; she liked to watch people's behaviour when they believed themselves to be alone, it told one so much. After a moment she laid down her pen and advanced with outstretched hand and charming smile.

She saw a woman who had yielded unreservedly to the claims of middle age. Cissie Getaway judged her to be the wife of a vicar in some provincial town. She had that look of utterly respectable and unseductive attractiveness which is to be found nowhere else in the world; the look of simple goodness, to which the navy costume, the frank, unpowdered face, and the thick grey silk stockings of a fashion thirty years old all contributed. Cissie Getaway took to her at once.

She was a Mrs. Roach, a widow; she had a letter from the Almoner of King William's Hospital to introduce her. The Almoner very much hoped that Mrs. Getaway would be able to help her, Mrs. Getaway being on the Board of a certain convalescent home for Indigent Gentlewomen, and Mrs. Roach being undoubtedly a gentlewoman and decidedly indigent.

Mrs. Roach had been hospitalized, as the Americans say, for eighteen weeks.

'Everyone has been so kind,' she said.

This nice woman had been Warden of an Old People's Home in South London for two years. She had loved the work, loved making the dear old souls comfortable and keeping them happy; it quite broke her heart to leave them. The trouble was that the Home was wretchedly understaffed; they just could not get people to do the work, and time and time again Mrs. Roach herself had been obliged to undertake the duties of linen maid, secretary, resident nurse, and even cook, besides her own work; till at last she had collapsed from sheer overwork. And now the doctors forbade her to undertake anything so arduous again.

It did not surprise Mrs. Getaway to hear this. The woman was plainly the sort of person who gave of herself unsparingly and never counted the cost. The pity of it was that Mrs. Getaway could do nothing for her. According to the terms of the endowment, as she explained, the convalescent home was solely for post-operational cases, and for this, alas, Mrs. Roach did not qualify.

Mrs. Roach sat on for a moment in the deep chintz chair as though too weary to move. Her blue clear eyes continued to look straight at Mrs. Getaway, but not as if she saw her, rather as if she brought all her fortitude to meet something very unpleasant. A kind of grey flush seemed to pass over her face.

Then she stiffened her muscles and forced herself to rise.

'It was so good of you to see me,' she said in her quiet way. 'I mustn't take up any more of your time, then.'

'You look so tired, my dear. Won't you sit down again and let me give you a cup of tea? Perhaps there is some other way in which I can help you?' Mrs. Getaway said.

'I shouldn't trouble you with my troubles.'

Poor woman! She had been over forty when her husband died — uninsured — and left her penniless, and quite untrained for any sort of work. If it had not been for the war, one wonders how she would have existed. She had no one behind her, and no home. There was nowhere now for her to go.

'What shall you do, then?'

Faintly, Mrs. Roach smiled. The absurd questions people asked!

'I don't know.'

'How much money have you?'

'Two pounds.'

'I mean, altogether, with your savings.'

'Yes. Two pounds: those are my savings. Being ill ate up my poor little nest egg dreadfully.'

'But, my dear, what are you going to do?' Mrs. Getaway insisted. One could almost think the woman did not understand her position, could not grasp that she was on the edge of starvation and penury.

Mrs. Roach bent her head and stroked her yellow scarf.

'The Lord will provide,' she said.

At the words, a thought darted like a goldfish into Cissie's mind.

'If you could get some light work in someone's home . . . ?' she suggested.

'Oh, I'd scrub floors!' the woman said eagerly. 'I don't mind what I do. I'm not afraid of hard work — provided my strength holds out.'

A slight frown ruffled Mrs. Getaway's creamy forehead at this impractical attitude, but she only said, 'Leave me your name and address, anyway; I may hear of something.' No use saying more until she had spoken to Aunt Luna.

★ ★ ★

Clouds ragged across the open archway of heaven. And just as Mrs. Roach descended from the Green Line coach, the wind rained down a gust of brown leaves. She waited on the grass verge, holding her breath, turning her face from the dust, till the wild spite of the wind had spent itself, then she crossed the road and went slowly up the rutted lane — noting, with the little pang autumn always brings to the elderly, how brightly the hips burned in the hedges. Like lanterns, she thought, fairy lanterns. She must tell that to Eleanor.

The lane wound uphill, and she paused at the gate to get her breath. Incongruously in the middle of harsh grey fields and bowing trees, stood a neat pebble-dashed bungalow with a beautifully kept garden like a drawing-room carpet behind its fences.

Through the bottle glass in the door, Eleanor saw her coming round the gravel path, and opened to her before she reached the step.

In silence the two women embraced.

'Dearest!' said Eleanor.

'How is he?' asked Mrs. Roach. Both women spoke in an undertone.

Eleanor sighed deeply, searching for words to describe just how he was. Not worse. She could not honestly say he was any worse. But, oh, sometimes *so difficult*!

'He knows I'm coming?'

'Of course. He's quite looking forward to it,' Eleanor lied. 'It always does him good to see you. Ah, how wonderful it is to have you here for a few hours again,' she sighed.

Mrs. Roach gently smiled acknowledgment.

The two women had met during the war, when both were working in the same department of Censorship. While Mr. Fielding was in hospital after the Fieldings' flat was blitzed, Mrs. Roach found Eleanor room in the same house as herself. That was the beginning of their friendship. Mrs. Roach was a tower of strength to Eleanor in those wretched days. For Eleanor luckily had been at work when the flat was hit; but her father, having been fire-watching the night before, was in his bed asleep; and woke to find himself trapped by the legs. It took them nearly three days to get him out.

He pulled through, more was the pity. Some people ought not to live after disaster. Mr. Fielding had hardly been an easy character at the best of times: a tetchy, sarcastic man, a typical schoolmaster.

Now he was left with a grudge against the world as well. When he was discharged from hospital, his daughter of course was obliged to resign from Censorship to look after him. It was essential to get him out of London, they said; so really she was fortunate to find this little bungalow at Edenbridge. There they had been ever since, sickeningly tied. Dreadful for him, but worse for her. Really, one could not have blamed her if she had murdered the old devil.

The last two years had been worse than ever.

The old man, now nearly eighty, had gone blind. Half-dotty with resentment, he was not even *nice* to his daughter. She stuck it doggedly, because it was her duty. She could never leave him, never, not even for a night; the hopeless Andromeda for whom no Perseus would ever come. She had nothing to look forward to but his death.

If it had not been for Mrs. Roach's letters, if it had not been for their hopes and plans together, she often thought she could not have gone on.

He sat in his wheelchair by the window, his hands wearily resting on the rug over his knees.

'Father,' Eleanor said, touching his sleeve, 'here is Norah.'

He did not trouble to turn his head. Only a derisive smile curled his lips as he said: '*Non cuivis homini contingit adire Corinthum!* Eh, Mrs. Roach?' He knew she would not understand and he hoped this greeting might embarrass or even offend her. He despised her. And it amused him, it always had amused him, to wound people with his tongue.

He could not see his daughter's faint pleading shake of the head, or her friend's reassuring smile. He only heard Mrs. Roach say quietly: 'Latin must be a great comfort to you, Mr. Fielding. I have often wished girls were taught Latin when I was young. All those wonderful old writers!'

Mrs. Roach sat with him while Eleanor prepared the dinner, and brightly, unflinchingly, chatted to him of this and that, of her journey down, of how the countryside was looking. He made no comment. He might not have been listening.

'Perhaps you would prefer me to read the paper to you?' she said at last, fatigued by his obstinate silence.

'No.'

'Oh, has Eleanor found the time to read it to you already? What a marvellous person she is!'

'Reading me 'the paper', as you call it, is not among my daughter's obligations, because it happens that I take no interest in the public prints.'

'No interest in world affairs? Now, you do surprise me, Mr. Fielding! I should have thought an intelligent man like you would always want to know what went on in the world.'

'Why should I care now what follies it perpetrates or what disasters it incurs? It has done its worst to me.'

'Oh, come now!' she chided brightly.

'Isn't that rather a selfish and personal way of looking at things? There is surely so much to be found in life if we will only try to widen our horizons.'

'My good woman,' he said, with a note of hatred in his dry old voice, 'what are your horizons to me?' After a moment he added huskily, '*Ad ripas Stygis Charonem exspecto.*'

'Please, do tell me what that means,' she said prettily.

He turned his angry useless eyes toward her.

'I am waiting on the banks of the Styx for Charon.'

'Oh dear! Will you be very shocked if I confess that I still don't understand?'

As though she were a dunderheaded pupil, he explained contemptuously: 'Charon is the boatman who ferries the souls of the dead across the river dividing this world from the world of shades. On the banks of this river I await him, with longing.'

She was — as he had expected — shocked by this.

'You shouldn't talk like that, Mr.

Fielding. You have so much to be grateful for. Think of Eleanor,' she reproved him.

'Well? Wouldn't it be better for Eleanor if I were dead? Why be afraid of the truth? What am I but a disagreeable burden to her?'

'You wrong her, if you think that. I have never heard her complain. I'm sure she doesn't feel — I'm sure she doesn't even *think* of you as a burden. She is *so* good, *so* loving. And here you live in this lovely spot. Why, one should be so grateful just to be alive!'

'Do you call this being *alive?* Helpless and useless, dragged about like a guy in its box? I'm so sick of it!' he snarled. 'Why can't I die?'

'All our times are in God's hands, Mr. Fielding.'

'You speak to *me* of God!' he cried, with a laugh of such savagery that she was quite startled.

When at length the midday meal with its embarrassments was over and the old man had fallen into sleep, Eleanor escaped. She plunged into her old tweed coat and the two friends went out into the brisk autumn sunshine.

'Oh, to breathe again!' Eleanor exclaimed, lifting her head for the wind to toss her grey-streaked hair. 'I only seem able to breathe when you are here. If only you could be here always, how easy it would be!' She sighed.

'I'm afraid your father wouldn't like that very much.' Mrs. Roach smiled. 'My stupidity irritates him.'

'It isn't you. He despises all women.'

'It's an inferiority complex.'

The women looked at each other knowingly and laughed. They caught hands, like girls, and went through the little gate at the bottom of the garden into the field beyond, the grasses leaving streaks of late dew on their shoes.

'You can't imagine what these moments of freedom mean to me.'

'Can't I?' Mrs. Roach said gently.

Eleanor turned harried brown eyes to her.

'Shall we ever be together, do you think?'

'One day,' Mrs. Roach promised tenderly.

43

'Dearest, if I hadn't that to look forward to . . . '

'And I,' Mrs. Roach admitted with beautiful candour; for she too longed for that day, as the soul yearns for paradise; for the day when Mr. Fielding was dead and she and Eleanor could share the neat little bungalow, and keep a few hens perhaps, and some bees: a home of her own again and never more anything to worry about financially — Eleanor would look after her. For, although she was conventionally shocked and even a little grieved at the idea of Mr. Fielding wishing for his own death, yet she wished for it just as ardently as himself. She was waiting just as keenly for Charon to fetch him from where he waited so impatiently on the banks of that dark river. All three of them wishing for his death — and the old man could not die!

'And all this while,' Eleanor said self-reproachfully, 'I haven't asked you a word about yourself or what you've been doing.'

Eleanor wanted to be told *everything*. Mrs. Roach selected the cheerful bits and spun them out to make them sound a lot. Not for the world would she have told Eleanor how broke she was. She had enough to bear without her best friend's worries. So Mrs. Roach talked brightly about Mrs. Getaway.

'She speaks of finding me a little job.'

As if she had suddenly arrived at a decision Mrs. Roach unpinned her hat and laid it on her knee (she was sitting on a stile, with Eleanor on the crossbar at her feet, gazing up at her). She wore her grey hair parted in the middle and looped shallowly over her brow, like a grandmotherly cat.

'What sort of a job?' Eleanor asked suspiciously. 'You know they said — '

'Oh, but this could not hurt me. She is very keen for me to look after an aunt of hers; one of those rather cranky old ladies, I gather. It would at least give me a homc for the time being, she thought.'

'I suppose it would be better than nothing.'

'Oh, I shall take it. I cannot afford to refuse.'

'And something better is sure to turn

up before long. Isn't it?'

'Now, I forbid you to worry about me,' Mrs. Roach said playfully. 'It will make me wretched if I think I am adding to your troubles.'

'How could you? What would my life be if I hadn't the thought of you to support me, with all your sweetness?'

She laid her forehead for a moment against Mrs. Roach's knee.

'You mustn't feel sorry for me,' Mrs. Roach said, stroking Eleanor's rough hair. 'You know I like old ladies. I'm really very lucky, aren't I? There's always so much to be thankful for.'

'Lucky old lady, whoever she is. I hope she's going to pay you well,' Eleanor mumbled.

'She won't pay me at all,' Mrs. Roach answered with exact truth.

At this Eleanor became indignant.

'Why should she expect you to look after her for nothing? It's not right!'

'If it is what God wants me to do, it is right: I needn't bother my head about anything else.'

'You're *so good!* I shall never be like

you; you're a saint!'

'What nonsense! Dear, if ever anyone was a saint, I know who it is,' Mrs. Roach said cryptically, with a tender look. And, because the prayer of a righteous woman availeth much, she added: 'Pray for me, tomorrow,' (that being when she was to see Mrs. Rampage, the cranky old aunt).

'She'll love you,' Eleanor said. 'I shall be so jealous.'

'I pray I love her too,' Mrs. Roach said humorously.

'But not too much. Promise you won't love her too much!'

'Silly child!'

'You might like her better than me. You might like it there so well that you'd decide to stay forever,' Eleanor said, half-sincere in her morbidity. But Mrs. Roach laughed and, catching her hands, pulled her to her feet.

'Write to me!' Eleanor cried, as the bus whirled Mrs. Roach away.

3

Mrs. Rampage had intended to make something specially delicious for supper as Henrietta was coming, but she dribbled away the hours and then was too tired to bother, and in the end she just opened a tin of sardines, messed it up with some leftover cabbage which was still quite fresh, and served it on toast with a dash of Worcestershire sauce.

She said, Did Etta mind eating in the dining room (which was chilly at this time of year)? And when Henrietta saw what it was, she agreed it was not worth the trouble of carrying upstairs to the sitting-room fire.

The dining room was in the basement, next to the kitchen; a long, dark, gruesome room lit by a grating in the pavement above the window. Mrs. Rampage had done wonders here. The grim little area outside the window she had walled with imitation ivy and made into a niche for a darling bronze boy with a fountain on his head. When the concealed lighting was turned on and the waters were playing it was an enchanting spectacle.

It wasn't on this evening. It was too expensive for everyday use, and anyway Henrietta had seen it dozens of times. But without that glowing picture it was dreadfully depressing; the dining room was dark and lifeless, and one gazed on to some dead-looking ivy coated with London grime.

Earlier in the day, luckily, Mrs. Rampage had slopped down the street and bought half a dozen cakes — rich ones, bursting their sides with cream. She could not get over it that they had cost ninepence each! All very well for Henrietta to remark acidly that good food did cost money; but it was like eating *gold*, she said, licking her fat fingers. Henrietta enjoyed them too, which was something.

This strange meal disposed of, they went upstairs.

'We don't need the light on,' Mrs. Rampage said, poking the sitting-room fire so that long streamers of flame flickered up the chimney like seaweed.

'No. More restful . . . '

Henrietta's brandy warmed on the hearth. Firelight on her face cast shadows like charcoal drawn on rough paper — a net of soft little lines down her cheek, a scribble at the corners of her eyes, and fierce black smudges for her capacious nostrils; the fire's rich glow on her dyed hair made it a quite believable amber.

Mrs. Rampage's brandy was held rather greedily between her short fat hands, turning it to catch the aroma. She liked to feel it, to hold it; she had restless little hands, always touching things for comfort.

They sat at their ease, with their skirts turned back and their knees wide so that the warmth could run up their thighs. Henrietta was worrying about a Worcester plate she had bought for genuine, and which Luna now said was the wrong blue. The more she thought about it, the more she believed Luna was right.

'Don't think about it, then,' Mrs. Rampage lazily. 'What's it matter? You can sell it all right.'

'Only that I paid Worcester price for it.'

But Mrs. Rampage couldn't be bothered to go maundering on about a plate. She had her own troubles. She was irritably unsure now of her decision about this Mrs. Roach.

'Am I cutting my own throat, I wonder?'

'Now what?'

'It may get on my nerves, someone hanging around me all the time.'

'I thought it was all settled.'

'I said she could come; we could try it . . . '

'Try it,' urged Henrietta.

'I could easily put her off, tell her I was going away . . . '

'Ducky, you're working yourself up over nothing. Give it a trial. You can always get rid of her later if you don't like her; you're not marrying her.'

Mrs. Rampage snickered feebly and took a sip of brandy. 'I've got cold feet,' she confessed. 'I've got my own funny little ways of doing things, and I don't want anyone interfering with them. I suppose I'm a fool.'

'You *are* a fool. I think it's a snip.'

'In a way.' Willing to change the subject now, she picked a little leather case off the sofa table. 'Did I show you my seals?'

'You did.'

Mrs. Rampage opened and closed the lid absently once or twice, watching the firelight spark on the stones.

'It'll do you good not to be alone.'

'Oh, pooh! After all these years!'

'That doesn't make it any better. And I always say,' Henrietta went on sagely, 'that it's worse for widows than for spinsters.'

'Well, good God, Ett, you're not comparing this stodgy old female with a husband, I hope? I'm not saying I wouldn't marry again if I got the chance.'

'Well, of course, dear. Who wouldn't? But this is different.'

'That's what I'm saying. Ett, you're not drunk, are you?'

This, Henrietta did not deign to answer. She said after a minute, 'But you'll have someone to look after you, and that's what you need.'

'Why?'

'My good Luna,' Henrietta laughed, 'if you don't, what on earth made you engage her?'

'God knows,' Mrs. Rampage muttered, uneasily trying to recollect. 'I can't think what came over me. I must have been sorry for her. She is a lady.'

'So am I, but I haven't noticed that ever made anyone sorry for *me*.'

But a lady was the last thing Henrietta looked with her passionate, raddled old face, a cigarette dangling from her lip, and her skirts pulled up. Indeed, the pair of them, glooming over the fire — Mrs. Rampage with her pallid witty face, and her frizzed hair falling on to her dowager's hump — resembled Carpaccio's courtesans rather than ladies.

'She's 'good family', come down in the world. Her father was Brigadier-General — Chough, I think she said the name was. Anyway, he was some big shot in India.'

'Never heard of him,' Henrietta declared.

'Oh, the Indian Mutiny or something,' Mrs. Rampage said vaguely. 'Anyway, the family came over with William the Conqueror.'

'Bloody old snob you are, Luna.'

'Easy enough to look that up.'

'Well, all that's ancient history. Who cares? What about her husband?'

'She hardly mentioned him; I gather he wasn't much use.'

'Impotent, do you mean?' Henrietta inquired, with interest.

'My dear, I never thought to ask. How remiss!' Henrietta laughed.

'You'll be able to have cosy chats about it on the long winter evenings, comparing notes.'

'Charles was anything but impotent. As you should know.'

'Why do you say *I* should know?' Henrietta said quickly, and her eyes flashed in the firelight.

'Oh, Etta, you can't have forgotten the hours you used to spend chatting to me while I sat in the bath drinking gin and nutmeg . . . ' Mrs. Rampage stuffed her fist against her mouth and said through her laughter, 'The time he found the empty bottle under the bath . . . he thought . . . I said the grocer sent round the spirits of salts in it . . . '

'I remember the time you sprained your ankle jumping off the lowboy,' said Henrietta, wiping her eyes.

They sat there laughing at past misery and forgetting the present.

'Oh, God, those were the days! What fun we had, even when it was awful! And now all I've got is this dim soldier's daughter to keep me company,' she groaned. 'Perhaps her husband *was* impotent. Perhaps that's what's wrong with her.'

'Why must anything be wrong with her? You were saying how nice she was a minute ago.'

'Everyone has something wrong with them.'

'Luna!'

'So a doctor told me once,' Mrs. Rampage said, spreading her short fingers complacently against her lap. 'Anyway, she hasn't got any children, because I asked; and she put on a face like *this* and said, 'No.' I thought she might have had them and lost them and I didn't want to hear about their gruesome deaths, so I didn't say any more. But of course if he was impotent, that may have been the tragedy. Yes, I expect that was it. And the silly fool — *dee mortibus* and all that — wasn't even insured when he died, so he left her penniless.'

'When was all this?' said Henrietta, with a yawn that cracked her jaws. 'My bye-byes,' she said, patting her hair.

Mrs. Rampage began to laugh again.

'Oh, Ett, she nearly made me yell. When I asked her how long she'd been a widow, she said, 'I buried my husband fourteen years ago,' as if she'd dug his grave with her bare hands in the back garden!'

'She may have, if she murdered him.'

'Do you think she could have? Ett, how grisly!' Mrs. Rampage looked over her shoulder into the dark. 'I wish you hadn't . . .'

'Let's have just another little drop; I've got quite cold. And then I must go.'

'Mrs. Roach would say 'chillsome',' Mrs. Rampage said, fetching the bottle. 'She's got a vocabulary to set your teeth on edge. You can see the clichés coming for miles. That's going to drive me mad, for one thing. She was telling me how she'd never been brought up to lift a hand, so I said, 'Oh, it's the same for all of us today!' Oh, she wasn't *ashamed* to work, she said; if she could lighten the burden for some weary soul, that was all she asked.'

'Crikey!'

' 'Well, so long as you don't try to be a bloody little ray of sunshine to me,' I said.'

'You didn't!'

'I damn nearly did, I promise you.'

'Never mind, Lu, it may not be as bad as you think,' said Henrietta, standing up and stuffing her figure into place inside her clothes. 'And anyway, she won't be costing you anything.'

'Not costing me anything!' Mrs. Rampage said in amazement. 'How do you make that out?'

'Didn't you tell me you weren't paying her?'

'Well, good gracious, Ett, what can you be thinking of? There's her keep, isn't there? Laundry, and lighting, and food! At *least* two pounds a week, I should say.'

'Not if you feed her on cod skin and

cabbage stalk,' said Henrietta, but she was painting a Cupid's bow on her mouth and did not say it aloud.

★ ★ ★

Mrs. Rampage's blood ran cold when she saw Mrs. Roach arrive with five enormous cabin trunks. Did the woman think she was going to stay forever?

'Goodness!' she said. 'I don't believe you'll be able to get them in your room. I'd no idea!'

'Oh, they can go anywhere, out of the way; any odd corner will do, Mrs. Rampage.'

'There really isn't . . . They *could* go in the cellar, I suppose. We do keep things down there. It's quite clean.'

'Oh, anywhere, Mrs. Rampage. The trouble is, if one hasn't a home, one is obliged to carry one's few belongings round with one, like a snail.'

'Better really to put them in store.'

'But, you see, they are all things I more or less need. I do hope you don't mind too much.'

'Oh, no, it doesn't matter a bit,' Mrs. Rampage said in a false voice.

'Because I'm afraid I've got something much worse than that to confess,' the woman said archly.

'Oh!'

'It's very wicked of me and I ought to have told you before. I ought, I *should* say, to have asked you if you would mind,' she corrected herself. She waited with her head on one side.

'Mind?' Mrs. Rampage was obliged to say at last.

'Would you mind *very* much if I brought my little cat here? She's very good and very clean,' Mrs. Roach added quickly.

'A cat!' cried Mrs. Rampage in dismay.

'Oh, do you dislike them?'

'I adore them. I adore all animals. I don't have one here simply because of the frightful damage they do.'

'Damage?' Mrs. Roach sounded mystified.

'Oh, don't I know them! Only the best Hepplewhite is good enough for the precious lambs to sharpen their darling claws on. And climbing all over the brocade chairs. Making their little messes on my Persian rugs . . . No, no, I'm sorry. I couldn't. I really couldn't.'

'Oh, but I shouldn't allow her into your rooms, Mrs. Rampage. Winky Woo is quite used to waiting in her basket in my room till Mother can take her for 'outies'. I promise you, you won't know she is in the house,' she said winsomely.

'Well, I don't think that's fair to an animal to keep it cooped up. No, I really am sorry, Mrs. Roach; but I think it would be better for us all if you made other arrangements.'

Mrs. Roach went quite white. She said nothing, just stood there like a fool.

'A pity you didn't think to mention it to me before,' Mrs. Rampage pointed out. 'But I expect you have friends who will look after it for you.'

'No,' Mrs. Roach said abruptly. 'I shall have to have her put to sleep.'

'Oh, dear! How dreadful!' said Mrs. Rampage, nervously fingering the balustrade, while she tried to think her way out.

'Better that than she should be unhappy.'

'Is it a terribly valuable animal?'

'Only to me,' Mrs. Roach said softly. 'She's just a little alley cat I happened to rescue. She loves me, that's all.'

'Oh, God!' thought Mrs. Rampage. 'Oh, God, what have I got into now? I can't tell the woman to go when she's just arrived, and anyway she hasn't got anywhere *to* go. And how could I face her here day after day with her cat's blood on my head? The guilt! The silent accusation! And I knew of a woman who went off her head when her dog was killed.' She saw Mrs. Roach coming for her with a carving knife, her pleasant face contorted.

'Oh, well,' she said weakly, 'we'll just have to see . . . '

From Mrs. Roach's Diary
Arrived here at 11:30 A.M. Taxi 3/9. Had a terrible fright to begin with when she said she could not have W. W. Dreadful moment. But I sent up a little prayer to St. Francis and he succoured us.

The old lady really has a very good heart. *If I can make her happy I am* sure all will be well. I shall soon settle in to her little ways.

The house is full of lovely things, like a museum. I have quite a nice little room at the top of the house, and when I have got my own things about I'm sure I shall feel quite at home. No bedside lamp and only a basket chair to sit in; one or two other things too I can see are needed. But it won't do to start asking for things before I've been here five minutes.

Now, is there anything I can do, I said to her straightaway. Not a thing, she said (she has a funny rather extravagant manner), dinner's all ready. I've only got to pop it in the oven; you run upstairs and unpack. When I came down she was reading the paper . . . One o'clock and not a thing done. She said she'd forgotten the time. She said, oh, I'm not a bit hungry, are you? I couldn't very well say I was. Living alone, I suppose she's got in the habit of eating just when she feels like it. I made myself *some Bengers. Here's a predicament right away. If I offer to get supper tonight, will she think I'm presuming? She made it quite clear that she did not expect me to do any cooking, and if I begin doing it, won't she expect me to do it always? I don't mind helping in reason but that was not what I was engaged for. Yet we must have regular meals. Perhaps she was just not feeling very fit today.*

Mrs. Roach did not mention any of this in her letter to Eleanor. There, all was splendid. She described the grass patch, the trees and the shrubbery — such a joy for Winky Woo! And there was a gardener called Peacock. Wasn't that a quaint touch? Mrs. R. herself was a delightful person, very active, and amusing. And she had a married daughter — only one child — a doctor, out in Malaya; they had spent the evening looking at snapshots of her.

What Mrs. Roach longed for was a home, somewhere where she could rest her weary soul, a place to fold her wings; and she believed she had found it here;

she prayed that it might be so: she was so tired. For such a place she would put up with any personal cranks.

And, Dearest [Mrs. Rampage wrote to Jonquil],

What do you think your old Mum's been and gone and done! I've got myself a housekeeper-companion — she's a perfect lamb, and runs up and down for me all day long — insists on giving me my breakfast in bed and altogether spoils me dreadfully. I expect she thinks I need taking care of!!! She had a brother who was out in Malaya, so she was very interested to hear all about *you*. Her father was Brigadier-General Chough. I got her through Cissie. I don't think Cissie is getting on too well with Wilfred these days — he apparently is always being *kept late* at the Ministry. I said to her — I didn't know they worked after five o'clock in the Civil Service. But — poor Cissie — it's too bad of him.

[There was then some gossip about a Mrs. Lawson, who doesn't come into this; a bit of 'cat' about Henrietta; and

64

a couple of paragraphs referring to Jonquil's last letter.]

Oh, we now have a rat catcher living with us. A female, name of Winky Woo! I call it Puss. The woman *adores* it. It's Mother this and Mother that, all day long. The day she came, the first thing she did was to sit down and put butter on its paws — which is a thing you do to cats to make them stay in a strange place, evidently. I nearly had a conniption fit. Butter, I said, out of 2 oz. a week!?! Oh, said she, I think she deserves a little treat after her ordeal (she meant the journey), and she does love butter. I said, so do I, but I don't think it penetrated.

Darling, you haven't told me . . .

Nevertheless, much to her surprise Mrs. Rampage found herself actually enjoying Mrs. Roach's company. Of course, she was rather a bore when she got on to India and the wonderful life she had known out there. It was something she loved to speak about, almost as much as Mrs. Rampage did about Jonquil. She seldom talked of her married life; it was as if all that had ticked away like the time does when one isn't looking; while her faraway girlhood was still as vivid to her as this morning's dream. But the best of her was that she was willing to listen.

To have someone new to whom she could boast about Jonquil was almost better than having Jonquil there herself, with her cruel impatience.

Before this, she had scarcely been aware herself how the silence of the empty house got on her nerves. Until Mrs. Roach teased her about it, she had not known she talked aloud to herself — telling herself in a running commentary what she was doing. Sometimes the radio ran on all day, just for the company; though she hated dance music and hadn't the patience to sit still long enough to listen to a play.

But with Mrs. Roach there was always someone to talk to. Or, rather, to talk *at*. And Mrs. Roach was so good, she never argued, never wanted to air her opinions. She maintained always a gently smiling decorum, a beautiful convent-bred latency. This decorous calm might unnerve Mrs.

Rampage in time to come, but at present it merely fascinated her.

One little thing only Mrs. Rampage disapproved of. Mrs. Roach was always — in Mrs. Rampage's words — 'running in and out of church'. Mrs. Roach was an Anglican, very High Church. And Mrs. Rampage hardly could have explained why she objected to it so much.

'I don't see how you can stop her,' Henrietta said.

'Well, I can't; I know that. But there's something about religious people, Etta; I don't know what it is, but I never feel I can really trust them.'

'It seems insincere,' Henrietta suggested.

'And yet, there must have been *some* good people who've been religious.'

Mrs. Getaway gave them a little time to settle down before she came to see how they were getting on. Aunt Luna quite raved about the woman. So that was one good thing. And Mrs. Roach herself of course could not sufficiently express her gratitude. Anyway, Cissie went off thinking that sometimes — just now and again — one organized something for people with really happy results, and those rare occasions compensated one for all the failures and frustrations attendant on ordering other people's lives for them.

Really, everyone was pleased.

Mrs. Roach got on almost too well with Lily Graveyard. Lily was quite absurdly devoted to her. She wasted Lily's time; that was what bothered Mrs. Rampage. She would hear them at it downstairs: interminable, morbid, antiphonal chants, like versicles and responses. And she would stump about rattily, hoping the noise would warn and disturb them; but not they! Even if she burst into the room where they were — Lily on her knees, perhaps, ostensibly laying the fire and Mrs. Roach with a duster in her folded hands — they did not start guiltily and bustle to their chores again, but went smoothly on as if she were not there, immersed in their long saga of disaster and disease (those ominous twins, shunned by Mrs. Rampage as a nun shudders away from the mere suggestion of sin). She would endure it as long as she could, fidgeting about the place, slamming drawers and twitching curtains into position, till at last the recital of horrors drove her from the room.

She told herself it was the waste of time that annoyed her so. There were surely plenty of little jobs that Mrs. Roach might have been getting on with instead of gossiping; and one could count the time Lily wasted penny by penny. It was not very amusing to think that every half-hour wasted by Lily cost Mrs. Rampage 1/3d. How would Mrs. Roach like that if *she* had to pay it?

But more even than the money, it was the gossiping she resented. She suspected them of discussing her behind her back, disloyally. She imagined afterward an attitude on their part of veiled contempt — pity and contempt.

All rubbish of course, she told herself briskly.

She did drop Mrs. Roach a word of advice about hindering Lily in her work — Lily was a great talker, she said.

'She really ought not to be working at all, with her back,' was Mrs. Roach's comment on that.

'What's wrong with her back, pray?'

'The doctors say she has a slipped disc.'

'Oh, if one listened to doctors!' laughed Mrs. Rampage, who only believed in doctors when it suited her. 'Don't encourage her, for goodness' sake, in the idea that she can't work.'

'It wouldn't be any use if I did, I'm afraid. What would become of her bedridden sister if Lily didn't go out to work? No, it's a hard case; the poor little thing certainly has her share of trouble.'

'They glory in it, that class,' Mrs. Rampage said easily.

Mrs. Roach said gravely, 'She was so upset this morning, she was weeping. It helps her, to get it off her chest a bit at my expense.'

'Hardly at *your* expense, I would venture to point out,' Mrs. Rampage laughed.

Mrs. Roach looked perplexed, not understanding what she meant.

'I mean, actually in terms of hard cash — when she wastes the time I'm paying her to work in, in talking to you, it is at *my* expense. In this way, I often lose as much as one and three or two shillings a day. It isn't the money I mind so much as the work carelessly done or left undone,' Mrs. Rampage said quickly.

If Mrs. Roach was shocked at this mercenary outlook she did not show it. She tried instead to explain that what had upset Lily that morning was her brother's youngest boy accidentally sticking the points of a pair of scissors into his eye — but she got no further than this when Mrs. Rampage, with a shriek, clapped her hands to her ears and ran away.

That was something Mrs. Roach could not understand: how anyone could run away from the sacrament of suffering, which was surely God's seal on those He had called to be His own. A strange and rather pathetic character, Mrs. Rampage, Mrs. Roach decided; she seemed to be afraid of life, always giggling and turning everything into a joke, as if that was the only way she could deal with it.

Mrs. Roach quickly discovered that there were always two subjects that could be relied upon to put Mrs. Rampage in a good humour: the first and the best, but also the most tedious, was her daughter

— she never tired of talking about her, rehearsing all her little clevernesses as a child; the other was her treasures. Mrs. Roach would get her to show them off to her and describe each piece: where it had been acquired and what it was worth and how much she had given for it.

Not that Mrs. Roach had any interest in it herself — but one could think one's own thoughts. It astonished her that anyone could lavish so much love and care on bits of wood or stone when there was all this misery in the world. But, in a flash of rare intuition, Mrs. Roach wondered if it were not to hide from this very misery that she absorbed herself in objects that could not change or suffer.

'To sell all one's goods and give to the poor,' thought Mrs. Roach (which is easy when one hasn't got any).

There was, for instance, her most prized treasure — which she kept locked in a cabinet. A shabby old casket that had once held somebody's love letters! With a crude painting inside of a man and a woman that Mrs. Rampage said was intended for Mary Stuart and Bothwell.

The way she went on about it! She had picked it up in a back street in Hastings for fifty pounds. This sum staggered Mrs. Roach — for an old box! But Mrs. Rampage said she could get four hundred for it any time she cared to sell. It ought, she said, to be in a museum. That this uninteresting little box could be worth so much fascinated Mrs. Roach, who used to come and stare at it in odd moments, wondering. Mrs. Rampage imagined she was admiring it. But it was the money she was thinking of — four hundred pounds! — and all *she* could do with it.

4

Mrs. Rampage was always losing things. Every day one heard her muttering, 'Where are my keys? Where did I put my keys? I had them in my hand just now. Where did I put them?' and then calling, 'Mrs. Roach, have you taken my keys?'

And Mrs. Roach would appear, unperturbed, 'Now, what would I want with your keys, Mrs. Rampage dear?' and find them beneath a rumpled stocking on her dressing table.

Or it might be money. Mrs. Rampage coming in from her shopping and discovering that she was a pound short. With mounting agitation she would add up what she had spent and count the money left in her purse, over and over again. It would not come right. A pound was missing! The fall of Troy could not have caused more anguished wailing!

Mrs. Roach would find it eventually tucked inside Mrs. Rampage's knitted glove. And Mrs. Rampage would put a hand over her mouth and laugh through her fingers guiltily.

But Mrs. Roach was used to old ladies and their funny little ways and she did not let it distress her. Even when Mrs. Rampage accused her of taking her nylons (or whatever it was), she did not get flustered. No, she pointed out quite reasonably and coolly that she never wore nylons so what would be the use of them to her? (Even in her agitation, Mrs. Rampage was too cunning to suggest 'Eleanor' and give herself away.)

Miss Graveyard, polishing the stairs, heard it all, and afterward came to Mrs. Roach to say, 'You don't want to let her upset you, miss. She's always going on like that, thinking people have took her things. I take no notice.'

'Nor do I, Lily,' Mrs. Roach assured her, smiling.

Sometimes, if it was something valuable, like a ring, Mrs. Rampage would be playful about it. 'It's no use, Roachy,' she'd say. 'Hand it over!'

Mostly the things turned up. But not

always. Some of the things Mrs. Roach had never even seen, evidently mislaid before her time, or she simply had not remarked them (she could hardly be expected to know how many hand-embroidered sheets Mrs. Rampage owned). But, as Mrs. Roach pointed out, Mrs. Rampage's home was so crammed with things, it was no wonder she could not remember exactly what she had or had not got.

This annoyed Mrs. Rampage, who insisted always that she knew exactly what she had got — even when she remembered later that she had sold it, or sent it out to Jonquil.

'Never mind,' Mrs. Roach would say consolingly, 'we all of us forget things as we grow older.'

A remark which astonished Mrs. Rampage the first time she heard it, for how was she different now from what she had ever been? In years, perhaps . . . but she never thought of herself as old; she didn't feel old, and surely she was still as capable as ever.

Yet there was no question but that Mrs. Roach regarded her as someone no longer perfectly able to look after herself. She ran up and down stairs for her, twenty, thirty times a day, to fetch her reading glasses or her purse or a letter. She saw to it that Mrs. Rampage had a proper rest in the afternoon with her feet up and a shawl over her.

One must have a heart of stone to reject so much kindness.

In these small ways Mrs. Roach hoped to make herself indispensable to Mrs. Rampage. It did more than that. Little by little it undermined the older woman's confidence in her own abilities.

'You shouldn't do that, Mrs. Rampage dear,' she was always saying. 'Leave that to me. You try to do too much. It's not right, at your age.'

How could one take umbrage, when it was meant so kindly?

And Mrs. Roach worried about her health and would nag anxiously, 'Are you *sure* you are feeling all right? No headache? You're not looking at all well. I wish you'd let me call in the doctor.'

At which Mrs. Rampage would laugh merrily and change the subject. (But afterward she could not help looking at herself in the glass uneasily and wondering . . .)

When Mrs. Roach was out Mrs. Rampage liked to scuttle up to her room and have a good look round. The woman was a complete stranger, she argued; what did she know about her? For all she knew, she might be a thief or a murderess. Not that Mrs. Rampage really expected to find a bloodstained chopper among her underwear; it was just her way of rationalizing her own crazy inquisitiveness.

She looked at *everything*. It gratified her childlike curiosity to see in the dressing-table drawer the tiny bottle of Odo-ro-no, the aspirins, hairpins and nets, the jar of cold cream and the weary old puff lying on a pot of orange face powder. They were not details she could have imagined for herself. She liked to stare at the photos in their silver frames: the Brigadier-General and his lady wife, the useless Mr. Roach, and a snapshot of Eleanor crouching by an Aberdeen terrier. She tried to read their characters from their faces. Was that mouth strong, or only hard? Were those kind eyes, honest eyes? It was difficult to decide.

There was a big wooden crucifix over the bed with a writhing Christ on it that she hated, but not as much as she hated the beastly little lamb that stood on the chimney shelf carrying a cross on its back. And she could not altogether avoid the coloured reproduction of the nun at prayer in her big white coif with a rosary clasped in her gnarled hands, or the photographic View over Jerusalem from the Garden of Gethsemane.

Once she had got past those, she looked for the letters. (That was how she knew about Eleanor.) She had seen a letter from her in the morning post, and as soon as Mrs. Roach went out she came up to see if she could find it.

She was hunting for it when Mrs. Roach said behind her: 'Are you looking for anything, Mrs. Rampage dear?'

Poor Mrs. Rampage jumped like a kangaroo.

Even the innocent look guilty if they are alarmed. Fear and guilt made Mrs.

Rampage attack straightaway.

'You startled me!' she said angrily, a hand to her bosom ('Hush, beating heart of Christabel!'). 'Creeping about like that!' she said indignantly.

'You quite startled me too,' Mrs. Roach said, with an unamused little laugh. 'I didn't expect to find anyone . . . in my room.' She glanced about quickly to see what had been touched. She could not bear the thought of anyone prying among her personal concerns. It was an outrage, a physical violation. A terrible feeling of being betrayed. Birds must feel like that when their nests have been tampered with, and they desert.

Mrs. Rampage said, 'I haven't touched — you mustn't mind — I like to see that everything's all right — just glancing round — ' She spoke a bit incoherently but without a blush. It was her restless old hands that betrayed her, running nervously round and round the edge of Mrs. Roach's prayer book.

'I hope you found everything all right,' Mrs. Roach said tartly.

Mrs. Rampage laughed uneasily at this

equivocal phrase.

'But you must be starving,' she said. 'I'll come down and get you something to eat.' She was so anxious to get out of the room that she almost pushed past Mrs. Roach.

Mrs. Roach was no fool. She *knew* well enough that Mrs. Rampage had been meddling with her things for some reason. 'If I had done such a thing to her,' she thought, 'then there would have been ructions. Funny the way people are. Thank goodness I keep my diary locked up.' She took it out of the suitcase under the bed and wrote in it: 'Very upset to find Mrs. R. in my room today, spying. Shall keep my door locked in future.'

★　★　★

Mrs. Rampage could hardly believe it when she went up the next day. She shook the door furiously. The ostensible object of her visit was to take Mrs. Roach a bedside lamp, out of the kindness of her heart, because she had noticed there was not one in the room.

She was on the way down with it in her hand when Mrs. Roach returned from the shops. Mrs. Rampage followed her in to the kitchen, where she found her unwrapping her purchases.

'Oh, steak,' said Mrs. Rampage, staring vaguely at the meat in its bloody paper that Mrs. Roach presented for her attention. She prodded it absently with her finger.

'I've just been up to put this in your room,' she said without preamble, 'and I couldn't get in.'

'Is that for me? How nice! I'll take it up when I run up with my things.'

'The door was locked.'

'Yes. I keep it locked now when I am not here.'

'You keep it locked? Whatever for?'

Mrs. Roach put her head on one side and smiled.

'One usually locks one's door to keep people out,' she suggested.

Mrs. Rampage, flushing to the eyebrows, declared that she had never heard anything so extraordinary in her life.

'I hope you don't imagine anyone is

going to take your things. Lily is scrupulously — She's been with me three years, and I've never — Not a thing,' Mrs. Rampage insisted.

'I made no suggestions about Lily.'

'Then what are you suggesting, pray? I'd really like to be told.'

'I'm not suggesting anything, Mrs. Rampage dear. It's just that I prefer to keep my room locked when I am not there. You surely don't object.'

'It's such a funny thing to do. Why? I mean, people *don't* lock their doors in private houses.'

Mrs. Roach looked at her in silence a moment and then said evenly, 'I've never had to before.' She could be calm because she was righteous; and she was determined not to be browbeaten by the little woman.

'Really, I wonder what you would think if I suddenly locked all the doors in the house and you found you couldn't get in! I wonder how you would feel? It's not a very pretty compliment to me, is it?' Mrs. Rampage was trembling with indignation and in an attempt to hide it from the other, she gathered up a handful of crockery to put away, but, too distracted to carry through an action, she dumped it on the dresser and opening a drawer began turning over the tray cloths with trembling hands and head bent to hide the angry tears.

'Please don't take it personally, Mrs. Rampage dear. It's not meant to offend you. Just think of it as one of my fads that I dislike my things being touched. We all have our funny little ways, don't we, and some of us are funnier than others.'

'And some of us are too funny by half,' Mrs. Rampage said rudely. 'I've never heard in my life of anyone going on like this. You seem to have the idea in your head that you can do just as you please here; I'm sure I don't know why you should think so. I knew this would never work; I told Mrs. Getaway so at the time. I shall explain the whole thing to her.'

'Why, Mrs. Rampage dear, what have I done?'

Mrs. Rampage slammed shut the drawer and caught the crockery again. It rattled uncontrollably.

' . . . out of the goodness of my heart,'

she stuttered angrily, ' . . . because you were ill . . . Cooking for you and everything . . . And what thanks? If my daughter were here you wouldn't dare speak to me like this!' A lump of self-pity stuck in her throat and nearly choked her.

Mrs. Roach was innocently amazed at the scene her little act of self-defence had provoked.

'But, Mrs. Rampage — ' she began.

'No! No, it's not good enough!'

Mrs. Rampage busied herself at the sink, still talking in angry gusts that were hardly comprehensible. She turned on the water so violently that it splashed all over her and dashed a cup out of her hands, and as she bent to pick up the pieces the iron frying pan standing beneath the sink fell forward agonizingly on to her shin. Tears of pain mingled with the tears of fury in her eyes.

'Better say nothing,' Mrs. Roach thought, watching from under her eyelids. Quietly, she began preparing the meal.

Mrs. Rampage darted forward and positively snatched the meat out of Mrs. Roach's hands.

'*Kindly* leave that meat alone! *I'll* deal with that, thank you!'

'Just as you please, of course. I was simply trying to help. It's already rather late.'

'We're not having this for lunch, as it *happens.*'

'I'm sorry. I couldn't know.'

'Exactly. That's what I said.'

'Am I to be told what we are having?'

'I don't know,' Mrs. Rampage said rudely. 'I haven't thought about it yet. I'm not in the mood for cooking. I shall probably go out to lunch. If I have anything at all,' she added.

Without a word, Mrs. Roach put the potato peeler back in the drawer. But even that was wrong, it seemed.

'I'm getting rather tired of cooking all day long for someone else,' Mrs. Rampage continued in an odd, high voice. 'The mistress of the house becomes the slave of the companion!' she declaimed extravagantly, with a parody of a laugh.

'That's not very kind,' Mrs. Roach remonstrated softly. 'You speak of gratitude; but I wonder who else you would find to do all I do without payment?'

'Why do you stay?' Mrs. Rampage asked cheerfully. 'The remedy is in your own hands if you aren't satisfied, you know; you can leave.'

'I'm not complaining,' Mrs. Roach began, when Mrs. Rampage burst in with great indignation: 'Well, my God, I should hope not! You've had nothing to complain about here . . . treated like a princess. I never heard in all my life — '

'I'm sorry you — '

'I don't speak about the cost of keeping you! But that I should be expected to run about all day long, waiting on you hand and foot . . . It's too much!'

Mrs. Roach looked bewildered, as well she might.

'Who does all the running about?'

'What do you think my daughter would say if she knew I had to clean the bath out after you?'

'Oh, Mrs. Rampage, *when?*' protested Mrs. Roach, laughing.

Without looking at her, indeed with her back toward her, as if she had not heard properly or had not understood, Mrs.

Rampage said: 'Well, go, then! I wish you would.' And she began clattering the saucepans together to put them away.

Mrs. Roach stood there, the smile fading out of her face as she steadied herself to meet this sudden blow.

'I'm sorry I haven't given you satisfaction,' she said at last, quite simply. 'When would you like me to leave?'

'Soon as you like,' said Mrs. Rampage, with her ostrich head in the cupboard.

'I shall try to find somewhere to go as soon as possible,' Mrs. Roach said humbly.

'Good, good, good!' Mrs. Rampage shouted rudely as she pushed past her (for she wanted to escape from the woman quickly, having cleverly brought the quarrel to this point) and tripped up over Winky Woo, who fled squealing, ' . . . that damned animal . . . filth . . . hairs. Good riddance! . . . Jonquil . . . ' she could be heard muttering as she thumped heavily up the stairs to the safety of her room.

Her heart was banging about inside her; yes, she was upset. For all her years of widowhood, it was beyond Mrs. Rampage's capacity simply to tell Mrs.

Roach to leave; she had never been able to dismiss an employee in the usual manner; there had always to be a towering scene to bring her to the point.

She kicked off her shoes and pottered about the room on her bunioned feet, muttering to herself between resentment and fear.

She caught sight of herself in the glass. 'Poor old Mum!' she said, sorry for her ugly red eyes and pink nose; and she popped a couple of sweets from the Sèvres bonbonnière into her cheek. Upsets always upset her, the poor old silly and on top of that, *no dinner*. A tear slid down her nose. She felt so sorry for herself that she could have burst into tears, but at that moment a stair creaked and, fearing it was Mrs. Roach pursuing her for further argument, Mrs. Rampage scrambled onto the bed, crammed a bar of chocolate into her mouth, pulled the covers over her head, and fell into righteous slumber.

Mrs. Roach felt so shaky she had to sit down on the kitchen stool for a moment. She lifted the cat into her arms and murmured into its fur. She would not take any notice of that silly, excitable old woman. Old ladies were often naughty-tempered and foolish, like children; and sometimes they needed a sharp fright as a warning; but sometimes it was best to ignore it entirely.

Mrs. Roach cut herself some fine bread and butter and made herself a beaker of Ovaltine and carried it up to her room: the row had made her quite peckish. She sat there with the eiderdown round her legs, doing her mending and singing hymns under her breath. After a while she took out her diary and wrote: *Today Mrs. R. gave me a lovely bedside lamp for my room.*

Just before four o'clock Mrs. Roach went down and laid a tray for Mrs. Rampage with a pot of tea and a lightly boiled egg and took it up to her.

Mrs. Rampage lay in the half-light with the quilt pulled up over her nose. When the door opened and she saw Mrs. Roach enter, she closed her eyes.

'Mrs. Rampage! I've brought you your tea!'

'I don't want any,' Mrs. Rampage said sulkily, and rolled over onto her side.

'Now, don't let it get cold,' Mrs. Roach urged, as she put it down and left the room.

'Damn!' said Mrs. Rampage, and sat up. She was streaked with chocolate like a schoolboy. She badly wanted her tea, and she never was one to resist the claims of her stomach. Afterward, she felt much better and a little ashamed of herself. She wasn't going to apologize (for that might lead to the woman thinking she could stay), but she might give her a little present to make up for her bad temper and the unkind things she knew she had said.

She considered a Minton vase with a crack in it that Mrs. Roach had once admired, but when she came to examine it, it seemed to her too pretty to give away, so she decided it wasn't good enough. There was a thin silver Queen Anne cream jug with an unmendable tear in its belly — but the worth of the silver alone, she thought, and popped it back in the drawer. Then she found a Dutch sabot in china, but Mrs. Roach wouldn't want that. At last she came upon a Carrickmacross table centre, rather badly torn at one edge. That would do nicely for Mrs. Roach's dressing table.

So Mrs. Roach was able to add to her diary that evening:

> *Had a rather unpleasant scene this A.M. with my old lady, all over nothing at all. I kept quiet till it blew over. I suppose she must have been afraid she had offended me, for later she gave me a beautiful lace table centre, Irish lace.*

Nothing more was said about Mrs. Roach going, and she didn't go. Mrs. Rampage quickly became reconciled to her remaining on because once more Mrs. Roach was running about and making her presence indispensable to her. She even took to calling her Roachy again.

Still, Mrs. Rampage would sometimes say, 'That's my handkerchief you've got there' (or 'my gloves' or 'my scarf that you're wearing'), but Mrs. Roach always replied quite calmly: 'No, dear, you're mistaken. I had this long before I came here. You must have one like it.'

'Well, where's mine then?'

'That I can't say,' Mrs. Roach would answer regretfully. This was one of the things she told the doctor when, just before Christmas, Mrs. Rampage caught influenza. She did not have it badly but Mrs. Roach insisted on sending for the doctor, saying she could not take the responsibility of looking after her otherwise; it was not fair to expect her to. This was the very opportunity Mrs. Roach had been waiting for — almost, one might say, praying for.

'Who asks you to take the responsibility?' grumbled Mrs. Rampage. 'I don't want to be nursed. I just want to be left alone. I hate people hanging round me when I'm not the thing.'

So Mrs. Roach left her alone. Mrs. Rampage came out on the landing and shouted for her in vain. She even climbed the stairs and banged on her door, sobbing with rage.

'I went out,' Mrs. Roach said mildly.

'You said you wanted to be left.'

'Leaving me to *die*,' Mrs. Rampage wept.

The doctor came, and listened to Mrs. Rampage's breathing; made a joke; and wrote out a prescription. Outside the door he was caught by Mrs. Roach looking solemn.

'Doctor,' she said in an undertone, 'how is she?'

'Oh, not too bad, not too bad. Have this made up, will you, and give it to her twice a day.'

'In water?'

'A little water. And keep her on slops for a few days.'

He issued these orders curtly as he ran down the stairs, the busy practitioner.

'When will you come again, Doctor?'

'Oh, you won't need me again; it's perfectly straightforward so long as she stays in bed and keeps her bowels clear.' He picked up his black trilby and settled it on his brow. In another minute he would have opened the front door and be running down the steps to his car. She hurried forward as if to open the door for him, and with her fingers on the handle, she said: 'I'm thankful you've seen her, Doctor, even though it's nothing serious. Lately I've been — well, *worried*. I don't feel I ought to have the responsibility of it all on my shoulders. It's not as if I were one of the family. If anything happened, they'd come to me and say I was to blame for not letting them know. But then if I told them, they wouldn't like it,' she said, with her earnest smile. 'It's one of those cases where one doesn't know what to do for the best.'

'Yes,' he said, not listening. 'Well, you let me know if she needs any further attention,' he said briskly, and reached for the door handle since she was making no effort to open it for him.

'Forgive me, Doctor, for keeping you. I know how busy you are. If you could give me just two minutes.'

'Certainly,' he said reluctantly.

'Will you come in here?' She led the way into the morning room and closed the door. 'Do sit down, Doctor.'

'No, thank you.' He had taken off his hat again but kept it in his hand.

'Cigarette? Now, I'm sure we've got

some somewhere,' she said, hunting along the chimney shelf and under papers.

'Not just now, thank you.'

'Well, do smoke if you want to.'

'Well, now, what's the trouble?' he said briskly.

'I hardly know myself.' She gave a faint laugh. 'You see, I've only been here six weeks. I was asked by a member of her family to come and look after her. I wasn't told that there was anything wrong with her — well, *mentally*, shall I say? — and now I wonder what I ought to do. She doesn't seem to realize it in the least, you see, but she does things or says things and then forgets she's done them.'

'Oh, we all get a bit forgetful as we grow older.'

'Yes, of course, Doctor. I think it's something more than that, though. Half the time she thinks my things are hers. I have to keep my bedroom door locked or she'd be in there when I wasn't looking, taking my things away and declaring them to be her own.'

'A touch of senility?'

'Well, is it that, Doctor? That's what I

want to know. Is it something that's going to get worse; that the family ought to be told about? That's where I need your advice.'

'I'd need to know a great deal more than that before I could tell you anything, I'm afraid.'

'Naturally, Doctor. I thought perhaps you could make an excuse . . . '

'I'll give her a look-over when she's better,' he promised.

'Thank you so much, Doctor, it will be a weight off my mind. Do you think it's serious?' she could not forbear to ask.

'We'll hope not,' he said in the cheerful, uncaring way doctors have, as he hastened off.

He came again a week later. Mrs. Rampage was up and about.

'The doctor, dear,' Mrs. Roach said softly.

'Who? The doctor? I didn't ask him to call. I don't want to see him. Tell him I'm out,' she said, starting up from her doze.

'Now, now, now!' he laughed, coming in behind Mrs. Roach.

She laughed too.

'I'm better, Doctor. It would be a sheer waste of money — I mean, time, your valuable time . . . '

'Well, now we're here we'd better just see that it's left no nasty aftereffects,' he said, whipping out his blood-counter and wrapping the rubber bandage round her arm. 'Feeling better, eh?' he said, pumping. 'Any pains in the head?'

'Not now.'

'Were they frequent before?'

'Constant, I'd say.'

'How long ago was this?'

'When I was ill,' she said, surprised.

'Oh, I see . . . Do you suffer with breathlessness?'

'Only after running upstairs — as you might expect with a girl like me.'

'Let's see, how old are you?'

'Too old to tell,' she said smartly.

He glanced at the machine. 'Over sixty?' he suggested.

'How unkind!'

'A bit forgetful at times?'

'No.' She stared. 'Why should I be?'

'Good, good.'

He stared into her eyes through an

ophthalmoscope, banged her kneecap, and said, 'Yes. Well, there's not much wrong with you.'

'I don't see why I should pay you to tell me that, when I said so as soon as you came in.'

'You're paying me for confirming your own opinion,' he said with his quick, not unpleasing smile, as he made for the door. And Mrs. Rampage laughed in high good humour, because at her age attention from any man, even if he was only a doctor, was agreeable.

Mrs. Roach waited for him outside the gate, where she could not be seen by Mrs. Rampage even if she came to the front door to see the doctor off the premises.

He was already diving into his car as he spoke.

'She's in not too bad condition,' he said cheerfully. 'A little hardening of the arteries, as is only to be expected.'

'But this confusion in her mind . . . ?'

'That would be part of it. Symptomatic. Nothing to be done about that, I'm afraid.'

'Will it get worse?'

'It won't get any better.'

'Oh, dear! What ought I to do?'

'I'm afraid there's nothing you can do.'

'I mean, ought her family to be told? I feel the responsibility is really too much for me to carry alone.'

'It can do no harm. They'll have to know sometime.'

He switched on the engine and let in the clutch.

'And may I refer them to you, Doctor, if they want more precise information?'

He nodded and raised a hand in salute.

'Oh, thank you!' she cried, as the car began to glide away. 'Thank you, Doctor!' And her relief must have been great, for she was actually smiling as she went back into the house.

★　★　★

The next time Cissie Getaway came to see her aunt was early in January. She was relieved to see that the two women were still on good terms; they seemed to have settled down quite cosily together. Aunt Luna, she noticed, teased the other a bit sharply sometimes, but it was all in good fun and Mrs. Roach evidently understood that Aunt Lu meant nothing by it, for she always laughed too, quite pleasantly.

'And what's the news of Jonquil?' Cissie asked politely. 'Did you hear from her for Christmas?'

'Oh, my dear, she sent me the most wonderful palm-leaf book: I must show it to you. But that arrived early, and I've heard nothing since then of course.'

'Oh, yes, dear, you had a letter from her only this week,' Mrs. Roach reminded her.

'*Thank* you for correcting me; you would know best, of course.'

'Mrs. Rampage, dear! You remember me saying it was rather a long time since you heard, and you said a letter had come that very day while I was out — last Tuesday, I think it was.'

'You must be right,' Mrs. Rampage said suavely, and added: 'Why don't you pop round to your church for half an hour while I have a little chat with my niece?'

'There's a rather important christening there this afternoon, but I'll be glad to run up to my room and scribble a couple of letters,' Mrs. Roach declared brightly as she left the room.

'Aunt Lu!' Cissie said reprovingly. 'You shouldn't have done that.'

'What?' Mrs. Rampage said innocently. 'I thought she'd be glad of the chance to flump down on her knees and say her prayers to some statue; she's always making excuses to go round there. I suppose she's in love with the vicar, poor man; they're all the same, these middle-aged spinsters.'

'How absurd you are! And anyway, she's a widow.'

'I always think of her as a spinster. Besides, her husband was impotent.'

'How do you know?' Cissie said, with a refined face; she never liked it when Aunt Luna became coarse — which was her regrettable tendency.

'I was told,' Mrs. Rampage said daintily, since she could hardly admit that she had it on Henrietta's authority. Another notion had come into her head while she was speaking and she went on airily, 'Of course, I've no way of knowing that it *is* to the church she goes. I simply rely on what she tells me, and she doesn't always speak the truth. For all I know, she may secretly visit an opium den. That would account for the frequency of her visits, anyway.'

Cissie frowned.

'Yes, that was what I wanted to say. I don't think she liked the way you spoke to her about Jonquil's letter, Auntie.'

'She's a damned busybody. I wish she'd mind her own business.'

'She was only trying to help, dear.'

'The point is, it wasn't true. She drives me mad, always creeping up to me and saying, 'Isn't it a long time since Mrs. Bracebridge wrote?' or 'What's the news of Mrs. Bracebridge?' Every day, mark you. As though I could possibly hear as often as that. I tell her I've heard, to shut her up.'

'I expect she thinks you like to talk about Jonquil. She's awfully well-meaning.'

'Epitaph for an ass.'

To change the subject, Cissie said gaily, 'But I haven't told you my news yet. Guess what?'

'You're going to have a baby.'

'Darling, that would be news indeed,' she said drily. 'No, Wilfred's going to

South Africa. Isn't it nice? We think, for at least a year.'

'What fun,' said Mrs. Rampage. 'And you will be a naughty grass widow?'

'Oh, no; I'm going with him. I'm not going to be left out of the fun, don't you think it. They say Durban is heavenly.'

'Very hot, I believe,' her aunt said jealously.

'I do hope so.'

'You'll probably get quite thin,' Mrs. Rampage said with a disbelieving little laugh. 'And what about all your committees, how will they manage without you?'

'They won't of course,' Cissie laughed. 'I dare they'll all go to pot.'

'But you don't care. How sensible! When do you leave?'

'Friday week.'

'As soon as that? It must have been very sudden.'

'It's been such a wild rush, darling, I simply haven't had a moment to come and tell you about it before. Putting all the things in store, and then passports, clothes, inoculations . . . I can't begin to tell you.'

'A pity you didn't let me know before. I

might have been able to help you with your clothes. Jonquil says not nylon on any account. It's fatal for the tropics. She says — '

One could hardly hope to escape having Jonquil's wisdom and experience pushed into one's ears; but Cissie listened tolerantly and promised to remember her advice.

Mrs. Roach, of course, put her foot in it during tea by talking about India and the way one dressed there.

'But that was in the year dot,' Mrs. Rampage interrupted rudely. 'Nobody wears topis nowadays.'

Cissie saw Mrs. Roach flush: really, it was too bad of Auntie! Without pausing to think, she said quickly, 'Hallo, where are the seals? They were on the sofa-table last time I came.'

'There!' Aunt Luna said triumphantly to Mrs. Roach. 'You hear? They were on the sofa-table. Perhaps you'll believe Mrs. Getaway.'

'I only said, Mrs. Rampage dear, that I'd never seen them.'

'Well, now you see that you must have

seen them — often.'

'Not to notice, I mean. I'm not very observant, I'm afraid.' She turned to Cissie. 'Mrs. Rampage's beautiful things mean so much to her that I can't make her understand — '

'What's the use of saying that? They're not here. Where are they?'

'I keep telling dear Mrs. Rampage that they can't be lost; only mislaid.'

'They're sure to turn up,' Cissie agreed, more because she was not going to sit there and see the poor woman bullied than because she thought it. Aunt Luna was not being kind today. She would try to get Mrs. Roach alone and have a quiet word with her before she left.

Mrs. Roach also was anxious to have a quiet word alone with Mrs. Getaway if it could be managed. There was a good deal she wanted to explain.

When Mrs. Getaway went to wash her hands, Mrs. Roach intelligently made an excuse and followed her. There was a moment of quickening sympathy between them at this glimpse of mutual understanding.

'You know,' Mrs. Roach began deprecatingly, 'your aunt is getting very difficult.'

'I'm so sorry, Mrs. Roach. But you mustn't let it upset you. She doesn't mean anything by it, you know.'

'Of course I don't mind. I never mind anything she says, the dear old soul. But really she has been so peculiar sometimes that I had to call in the doctor the other day. I was worried that she might be going off her head, the things she says sometimes and does.'

'Why, Mrs. Roach, what sort of things?' asked Cissie, feeling cold at this crude phrase. (Could she have been mistaken in this woman after all?)

'It is a shame to have to worry you with this just when, you're off on your lovely holiday, but I feel it wouldn't be right of me to let you go unknowing — in case anything should happen while you are away.'

'God forbid!'

'Yes, indeed. I know how devoted you are to your aunt. That makes it all the sadder. And the doctor says it can only get worse with time.'

'What will get worse?' Cissie said quite sharply.

'Why, this loss of memory, this — this confusion about events, in her mind. Like the letter from her daughter that she had forgotten receiving. And you see she won't ever admit that she's wrong. And then those seals. I hate to tell you this, Mrs. Getaway, when you gave them to her. But they're not missing at all. She sold them. I couldn't tell you why. But she told me she was going to sell them, to Mrs. Purvis, I believe. Then she forgets, I suppose, or simply doesn't want to admit it, and pretends that someone has taken them — usually me, I'm afraid.'

'They were hers to sell if she wanted to; I wouldn't have minded,' the other said sadly. Poor Aunt Lu, she had not been half nice enough to her. How wretched old age was. 'Do you find it all too much for you, Mrs. Roach?'

'Frankly, Mrs. Getaway, if I wasn't here, there would have to be somebody else to look after her, the doctor said. She's really not fit now to be alone. Of course, if you think she'd be happier with someone else . . . '

'That was not what I meant at all, my dear. I simply meant did you feel you could cope?'

'I'm really very fond of her. Behind it all, she's a dear old soul,' Mrs. Roach said tenderly.

'A dear old soul' seemed hardly an accurate description of her aunt, but Mrs. Getaway accepted it gratefully at the moment, and was thankful the woman believed it.

'Then I can rely on you to look after things while I'm away?'

'Oh, you can depend on me,' Mrs. Roach promised, with her gentle, reassuring smile. 'I'll look after everything.'

5

Mrs. Roach could honestly see no wrong in using some of Mrs. Rampage's furniture to improve the appearance of her room and make it more comfortable. There were lots of odds and ends about the house that were lying shut away in rooms and never used. What harm was there in putting them where they were needed and could be appreciated? If she did not ask Mrs. Rampage's permission it was because she already knew her character well enough to know it would be useless. It was not that the old woman was ungenerous, but rather that the indication that another person wanted something she had ceased to value alarmed her into an immediate instinctive acquisitiveness. Asked for a specific object, she would always reply, 'No, I can't let you have *that* . . . I got it from — but you wouldn't want it really, it's not a good one. I'll let you have something much better,' and rummaging forthwith among her things she would produce something irrelevant to its purpose or grossly inferior.

Better, far better, and wiser, simply to remove what she wanted when Mrs. Rampage happened to be out of the house. And, as Mrs. Roach had said so often before, she had so much that she seldom required any of the things stuffed away in back rooms and attics, or noticed that they were no longer there.

Also, determinedly keeping her door locked obviated any trouble. If ever anything was said, she knew what she would reply. She'd say it was to make the room look nice when her friend came to see her. For Eleanor, after a tremendously elaborate piece of organization, was coming up to town for the White Sales, and would have tea with Norah before catching the 6.15 home. She would hate Eleanor to see the room as it was, so shabby and unloved, no better than a servant's bedroom. Indeed, not to be compared with the servant's bedroom of today, with its cosy armchairs and gay chintz covers and the little brown radio on the bedside table; but what she meant were the Victorian hellholes that were servants' bedrooms when she was a child.

When Mrs. Rampage heard that Eleanor was going to honour No. 5 with a visit she almost gave herself away with a cry of delight. However, she suppressed the sparkle in her eye, and merely said that would be very nice for Roachy.

'I'm afraid I shan't be at home,' she lied, 'but I'll try and get back in time to meet her.'

'Oh, please don't bother,' Mrs. Roach very nearly said; but it would be all right because she had chosen Friday on purpose, knowing it was the day Mrs. Rampage went to the hairdresser.

But Mrs. Rampage had no intention of missing such a treat; it would be unfair to Henrietta and Geraldine Lawson and her other friends, whom she had diverted with quotations from the letters, to miss the opportunity of describing to them the old girl's girlfriend in person.

Mrs. Roach was down in the basement cutting sandwiches when Eleanor rang the bell, and before she could wipe her hands and run up to answer it, Mrs. Rampage had darted out of the morning room, where she'd been sitting like a spider, and let her in.

'Come in, come in,' she said, laughing heartily, for no reason that Eleanor could see. She led her straight into the drawing room. 'You must be exhausted! I expect you'd like to take off your things, but it's no use me taking you up to Roachy's room because she always keeps it *locked*.'

She threw her an immensely roguish glance, laughing good-humouredly at Eleanor's bewildered expression, unable to follow her allusions. She struck Eleanor as being unexpectedly worldly and gay; not at all the Flopsy bunny, the rather doddery old dear, Norah had led her to expect.

Just then Norah came in with her shy smile and said, 'Oh, Mrs. Rampage, may I introduce . . . '

'Now, I know you two have got a lot to say to each other, so I'm sure you'll excuse me if I get on with my correspondence. I want to catch the mail, for my daughter in Malaya.' She could never resist the chance of talking about Jonquil to a stranger: there were shop assistants and bus conductors who knew as much about Jonquil and her whims and repulsions as, say, Henrietta Purvis. So she lingered for a few minutes, chatting gaily about her daughter's plans, talking at Eleanor as though Mrs. Roach was not in the room, and greedily observing as much as she could about this simple young middle-aged woman, with her shaggy, unfashionably dim tweeds, and the coarse threads like white cotton in her dark hair. Disappointing, really. The letters had led Mrs. Rampage to expect — well, she did not quite know what, but she was disappointed.

She scribbled off the rest of her letter and banged the front door loudly behind her when she took it to the post.

'I thought she was going to be out, dearest,' Mrs. Roach said apologetically.

'But she's nice, isn't she? A merry old thing, I thought.'

Mrs. Roach said nothing but looked worlds of benign resignation.

'Norah!' Eleanor cried anxiously (and yet she was ashamed to acknowledge a lift at the heart). 'I thought you liked her.'

'Poor old thing, one can't help but be sorry for her. She's not got a very happy temperament.'

'I should have said that's just what she had; she seems so cheerful and good-natured.'

Mrs. Roach smiled sadly.

'That was not quite what I meant, dearest; she has a rather unfortunate nature, was what I meant. She's like a certain little girl who had a little curl right down the middle of her forehead,' Mrs. Roach said whimsically. 'When she is good, she is very very good . . . ' She shrugged and forbore to conclude.

'I'm rather glad, I think, that I don't have to be too jealous,' Eleanor said shyly. 'I was a little afraid from your letters that you were getting a bit too fond of her.'

'Dear, I try to make the best of things.'

'Don't I know how brave you are!' Eleanor said impulsively, giving her hand a quick squeeze. 'Norah, what did she mean? She said something just now about not being able to take me up to your room because you kept the door locked. I thought it such a funny thing to say.'

'It was a very funny tiling for *her* to say. I should have thought she'd be ashamed!' And Mrs. Roach told her how she had discovered her, spying, reading Eleanor's letters (Eleanor blushed vividly). 'There you are! That's what she's like! And then she'll be sorry, like a child, and give me a present to make up. A woman her age! No, she's not like a normal person at all.'

All the same, she was fair to Mrs. Rampage, and while they were up in her room she showed Eleanor the presents Mrs. Rampage had given her. Eleanor once more felt a pang of fear and jealousy.

'She must be awfully fond of you,' she said.

'I think she is,' Mrs. Roach said complacently.

'You should have asked your friend to stay to supper,' Mrs. Rampage said on her return, peeping into the simmering pot where a calf s head gazed reproachfully up at her from jellied eyes.

'It's very kind of you, but she had to get back; she has an invalid father, you know.'

'Oh, you should have *made* her; it would have done her good.' It was a waste of time telling Mrs. Rampage some things; she just refused to let them into her head if they didn't suit her. Mrs. Roach could see that she would never accept the idea that Eleanor was tied to her father, so she said nothing more. 'I thought she had such a sad expression,' Mrs. Rampage said inquisitively. ('Like an Aberdeen terrier begging for a bone,' she added to herself.) 'Why did she never marry?'

'I've no idea.'

'But she must have been quite good-looking when she was a girl, I should think.'

'Yes; possibly.'

'Surely she must have had offers?'

'I'm afraid I really couldn't say. I've never asked her.'

'Oh, I thought she was a great friend of yours,' Mrs. Rampage said, lolloping brains out of the calf's head into a bowl.

Mrs. Roach turned her eyes away from this unseemly sight and said delicately that the greater the friendship, the more need for reticence; one must respect the soul's privacy.

But this rebuke went over Mrs. Rampage's noddle.

'That's not *friendship*. I'd like to see Henrietta Purvis respecting *my* 'soul's privacy'!' And she smiled, a secret, ribald smile.

'It does take all sorts to make a world,' Mrs. Roach said blandly, hoping this would end the conversation.

Mrs. Rampage, throwing a raw egg onto the brains and then mashing them about with her fingers, presently murmured: 'Is she clever? What does she *do?* Oh, didn't you tell me she lived at home? Then they're quite well-off, I suppose?'

'Really!' Mrs. Roach uttered a ringing laugh. 'What pity you didn't think to ask her yourself when she was here. I'm afraid such matters don't interest me very much.'

'Oh, no, *I* couldn't ask her, I'm a stranger,' Mrs. Rampage explained kindly.

'Though why people pretend they're not interested in money, I can't think. If you're not interested in it, it's no wonder you haven't got any.'

'Perhaps that *is* the explanation.'

'But if your friends are well-off, I wonder they didn't help you when you needed a home.'

Mrs. Roach flushed crimson and studiedly didn't answer.

'Oh, have I been tactless?' Mrs. Rampage said cheerfully. There was lots of fun to be had out of old Roachy one way and another.

One of the things which particularly vexed Mrs. Roach was the money Mrs. Rampage threw away on useless junk when she refused to pay for Winky Woo's few penn'orth of fish heads daily, and openly grudged Mrs. Roach the extra pint of milk that the doctors had told her she must take. It seemed such wanton waste, even though some days it would not amount to more than five or ten shillings for a pottery jar or a decanter label or a caddy spoon; things that one could not possibly want, in a house already stuffed like a museum with more than it could hold. And to aggravate the situation for her, she was always called upon to admire the new trophy Mrs. Rampage held in her fat little hand and gloated over. The fact was that she simply had no sense of values, no money sense at all — the very fault of which she accused Mrs. Roach. And this was proved clearly enough in the Peacock case.

People who come in daily to work so often have with them mysterious leatherette bags or parcels that Mrs. Roach thought nothing of it to see Peacock, the gardener, hunching off with what looked like a pair of boots wrapped in old trousers and half-concealed beneath the mackintosh flung over his forearm. They might have been part of his working gear.

'We're off now,' he'd say cheerfully, with his half-mad, guilty smile. 'Taking this old broom back to the wife. May get it thrown back at us,' he'd add, ducking his head and looking sideways ruefully, smiling, out of round caramel eyes. It was those eyes, in that round, brown, foolish face, together with the soft bush of hair, and the apologetic grin, that made one think of a cheerful teddy-bear.

'Well, I don't know,' she'd say doubtfully. 'Did Mrs. Rampage give it to you?'

'It's no good, see? We never use it.'

'I think you'd better just ask her though.'

'Right you are,' he'd say, quite good-humouredly. 'We'll ask her next time.'

Mrs. Roach just thought him simple-minded and harmless. He was not a very able gardener, but he kept the place tidy and he was always willing and cheerful. Wet days, he'd chop wood.

One damp afternoon, as she counted the shillings into his hand, she noticed a tidy bundle of firewood carried under his arm and partially hidden by the mackintosh tossed over his shoulder. She did not like to stare at it, but he saw the direction of her gaze and he threw a quick, furtive glance at her. He nodded and smiled reassuringly, and for the first time she noticed how watchful and uninnocent his simpleton's eyes were above his grin.

'Ta,' he said, slipping the silver into his pocket. 'Chopped you a nice lotta wood today,' he said conversationally. 'Stacked it all tidy. We're just taking home a bit of firing for Mr. Peacock: save the wife a job.'

'That's right,' Mrs. Roach said, because he seemed to expect praise or at least approval for this act, and she could not think even Mrs. Rampage would grudge a few sticks to her gardener. She had an idea that such trifles were a gardener's 'perks'.

A hundred yards down the road there was a street of small shops, which Mrs. Rampage went to for necessities. Mrs. Roach, having used the last of the bread for tea, was obliged to run down to the baker's for a small loaf before they shut. She took only the time to put on a coat and hurried out after Peacock, indeed, as she closed the gate, she saw him turn into the street at the end of their road and was faintly surprised, having always supposed that he turned right not left from No. 5 and caught a bus. Perhaps, like herself, though, he had some small purchases to make — to buy something for the children's supper out of the silver he had earned (and she went off into a dear little daydream about his shining cottage full of rosy-faced children, though God knew the mere sight of him in his deplorable garments was sufficient indication of his squalid background and slatternly wife and their ragged, snotty-nosed kids). If he had not been in her thoughts, she might not have noticed him, as she turned into the street, slipping into the oil shop. She hurried on, bought her loaf, and a moment later came face to face with him. She automatically glanced at his hands to see what he had been buying, but his hands were empty.

'Just hurrying off home,' he said guiltily. 'Mustn't be late, must we, or we'll catch it!' He laughed ruefully, ducking his head. He was watching her to see what she would say, but she merely nodded pleasantly and hastened on.

It was only afterward, after he had turned the corner, that the impression made on her brain informed her that he was no longer carrying the bundle of firewood under his arm. Again, she was mildly surprised, and on an impulse that she could hardly have explained to herself, she entered the oil shop (which smelled stiflingly of creosote) and put forward a question or two. Firewood was 2½d a bundle. Peacock irregularly brought in a dozen or so bundles at a time, which the oil merchant bought for a penny each.

Mrs. Roach was dismayed by such pitiful deceit, and shocked that the wretched little man could take on the sin of dishonesty for a mere handful of coppers.

It was his immortal soul that she was thinking of when she told the sad business to Mrs. Rampage. 'It's terrible to think of, isn't it?' she said compassionately. 'We ought to do something.'

But Mrs. Rampage only saw in this tale that she had been badly taken in by someone to whom she'd been kindness itself, often giving him heels of stale bread to take home or shrunken-up woollies for his children, and *this* was how he repaid her. Not only stealing her wood, which heaven knew one would think was bad enough, but actually chopping it in the time during which he was paid to work for her. She was being cheated both ways.

'Terrible?' she exclaimed. 'I should just

think it is terrible. I'll do something about it all right, don't worry. My God, I'll do something about it!'

'He must be in dreadful straits to do such a thing,' Mrs. Roach said charitably.

'He'll be in dreadful straits when I've finished with him,' Mrs. Rampage promised, her angry old hands pushing the china about the supper table with nervous gestures. She was in one of those blank rages where one can only stutter back another's phrases like a parrot. And her passion was aggravated by the suspicion that Mrs. Roach's sympathies were with that swindling wretch instead of with her, as in all loyalty and common sense they should have been.

'It was very wrong of him,' Mrs. Roach admitted. 'But perhaps if we can help him he won't need to do it again.'

'He certainly won't do it again to me, I can promise you.'

'Oh, dear! I hope that doesn't mean you are thinking of giving him the sack. I should be very unhappy to think I was responsible for the poor little man's losing his job.'

'You didn't really imagine I would keep him on!'

'Oh, now, Mrs. Rampage, you really do distress me. But you don't really mean it. You try to make yourself out to be harder than you are.'

'I'm the one that's distressed! It's been a terrible shock to me! When I think of the money he's cost me, I could weep . . . ' And her eyes did actually fill with tears which, to prove the sincerity of her feelings, spilled over and splashed onto her plate of tripe. (Her favourite supper! But how could she enjoy it now? It was ruined — though she gobbled it up with her tears in a frantic kind of way that boded dyspepsia.)

Mrs. Roach stared in amazement, having never seen any human being who could eat and cry at the same time. She leaned across and spoke to her as she would to a child.

'Only think, dear, if those few shillings mean so much to you, what they must have meant to him.'

The tone of this remark sent Mrs. Rampage into speechless, blistering fury, but Mrs. Roach went on smoothly: 'Give him a good talking-to, yes. I'm all in favour of that: he deserves it. But you couldn't sack him for such a trivial little crime, it wouldn't be Christian.'

'Well, if Christianity condones theft, thank God I'm an atheist!' Mrs. Rampage exclaimed.

'We don't condone, any more than we condemn: it is not for us to judge,' Mrs. Roach said, with just the right tone of wearily gentle rebuke.

' . . . that I should be preached to at my own table!' Mrs. Rampage ejaculated furiously, rising from it as she spoke and dragging the cloth along with her, caught in the folds of the napkin she still held in one hand. The woman was an idiot! One might have guessed she would see everything perverted.

'Oh, look out!' cried Mrs. Roach, flinging out a hand too late to prevent the plate from sliding over the edge of the table, followed by the coffee cup and the butter dish . . . 'Oh, my dear!' she said, hurrying round the table to her. 'Let me . . . I'll do it.'

But this was the straw too much. For Mrs. Rampage just then, the malignant forces of the universe seemed leagued against her. Tears of rage and despair gushed out of her eyes again, as if a button had been pressed.

'Oh, do get out of the *way!*' she cried impatiently, with a savage gesture that struck Mrs. Roach in the chest. 'It's all *your* fault!'

Mrs. Roach stood for a moment with her hand on her bosom reproachfully, like Botticelli's Venus, and then in silence retired.

'Why can't anyone . . . ' Mrs. Rampage sobbed, on her hands and knees among the broken china, trying to scrub out the coffee stains on the carpet with her napkin and using it from time to time to mop away her tears. The tripe kept dropping apart in her fingers as she tried to pick it up; it was as bad as trying to pick up jelly, and she was too overwrought to attack the problem intellectually and take a spoon to it. She rubbed away the mess with the ruined napkin. 'No one ever . . . ' She hiccupped dolefully, picking fragments of glass out of the butter — which one simply could not afford to waste in these times — and then wiping her buttery fingers on her skirt. 'If it was anyone else, they'd send for the police,' she argued. 'And I shall tell him so.'

But the opportunity for that did not occur. Mr. Peacock did not return. As it was winter, Mrs. Rampage decided she would not bother to replace him.

'I really can't afford to keep a gardener, with all my other expenses,' she told Mrs. Roach — meaning *her*, as Mrs. Roach perfectly understood.

It was precisely the day after this that Mrs. Rampage came in in high excitement. She had found for twenty-two pounds in the Fulham Road a treasure, a wonderful little piece by — Schlaken-something, it sounded like. Her small fat hands were shaking with excitement as she unfastened the wrappings.

On an ebony stand under a glass bell, Mrs. Roach saw a perfect little white china miniature of an eighteenth-century lady playing a clavichord. Even she could see, though she was not moved by, the charm and elegance of it: the grace of her gown ornamented with ruchings of the finest net and sweeping in lovely folds over the stool on which she sat, to the tips of her tiny rosetted slippers. The posture of her fingers and wrists above the keys of the little instrument and the serene 'listening' poise of her head betokened an eloquent performer. Someone more fanciful than Mrs. Roach might imagine that if only the glass case were removed and one listened very intently, one would catch the faint beguiling tinkle of the minute air she played.

'Isn't she adorable?' Mrs. Rampage groaned. 'Couldn't you eat her? And she's in mint condition, too. One of his pieces, a bit earlier it's true, went for three hundred and eighty pounds the other day. And I found her in a crazy old shop lying between a zither and a pot. Imagine it, only twenty-two pounds! Wait till I tell Henrietta, she'll murder me!' she chuckled.

Mrs. Roach stood there like a stock, with her hands clasped, thinking: Twenty-two pounds for a piece of useless bric-a-brac that could be smashed to fragments in an instant; and this was the woman who moaned that she could not pay the rates, and made a scene over the telephone bill, and turned away a poor, bumbling working man because he had done her out of a few shillings! Either the woman was mad or she was abominably cruel. Mrs. Roach positively trembled with indignation.

'Very pretty,' she said coldly, and left the room.

'Now what's she in a mood about?' Mrs. Rampage inquired aloud. 'I shall put the White Lady in my own room, where I can see her when I wake up in the morning,' she decided. And she very carefully carried the precious object upstairs and made a place for it on the Sutherland table between the windows. Whenever she bought something new, she liked to keep it near her, to pet and admire it and be comforted by its charm or beauty, like a child with a beloved doll from which it cannot bear to be separated. Now, the better to enjoy it, she got down on her poor old knees; and

Mrs. Roach, coming in to tell her that dinner was ready and seeing her there before it, thought, *The heathen in his blindness bows down to wood and stone!*

6

It was a piece of extreme good luck for Mrs. Roach that her protector, Mrs. Getaway, had left England. It made her feel more secure. And Mrs. Rampage's daughter was thousands of miles from home too. The only person close enough to be a nuisance was Mrs. Purvis, and she hoped to deal with her. She meant, if she could, to spoil the friendship by insinuating between them unkind words and thoughts, like a wedge which with gentle and persistent tapping will finally split a rock.

That was the theory of it, anyway. Practice is seldom what one expects, particularly so if one has plotted out action and reaction in advance. Mrs. Purvis snubbed her very rudely the one time she tried to be confidential about Mrs. Rampage; and she knew she had failed there. In fact, she had to guard against Mrs. Rampage learning about it, by saying in her wistful modest way, 'I'm afraid Mrs. Purvis doesn't like me,' and wasn't much helped by Mrs. Rampage answering: 'I don't suppose she thinks about you one way or the other, my good woman.'

'She's so quick-tempered, isn't she? She misunderstood something I said the other day and she wouldn't give me a chance to explain.'

'That's Henrietta,' Mrs. Rampage acknowledged, with a pleased smile; but Mrs. Roach did not understand that the vices of the people we love we only too often regard as virtues.

'I'm sure there's no need for me to be frightened of her. I expect under her brusque manner she's got a heart of gold.'

'I don't know about gold,' Mrs. Rampage tittered. 'If she had a heart of gold, I dare say she'd sell it and buy one of brass.'

Mrs. Rampage, then, had a funny idea of friendship. She apparently did not mind speaking maliciously about her best friend to a third person. And yet when Mrs. Roach, encouraged by this, ventured like Claudius to drop poison subtly in her ear, it seemed not to affect her in the least. It was as though, preoccupied with other images, these had not succeeded in imprinting themselves on her mind.

The truth, which was beyond Mrs. Roach's compass to grasp, was that Henrietta and Mrs. Rampage were as unsusceptible to misunderstanding as an old loyal married couple; not in any sense devoted to one another, they yet were completely familiar with the processes of the other's thought; and, even though they laughed at and despised each other over some things, it in no way affected their comfortable and undemanding relationship.

The odd thing for Mrs. Rampage was that, although she was so accustomed now to having someone in the house that she could hardly bear the thought of being alone again, Mrs. Roach's presence and her unswerving gentility irritated her more and more. Mrs. Roach's persistent daintiness set her nerves on edge. She spoke more and more rudely to her, but Mrs. Roach remained unfailingly polite and in command of herself.

'*Cockroach!*' Mrs. Rampage said to herself. She would work up a scene over nothing, without any help from Mrs. Roach, to the point where she could tell her to *go;* whereupon, Mrs. Roach would quietly say, 'Very well,' as though she meant it, thereby cutting the ground from under Mrs. Rampage's feet, and then simply never leave, never even make any attempt to go. It was maddening.

And then Mrs. Rampage had a brain-wave.

As usual, it was several weeks since she had heard from her daughter, and then she got a letter to say that after all Guy had decided that they could not possibly take leave in England this year. Mrs. Rampage's heart sank horribly. She had so *hoped* . . . The knowledge that she was going to see her daughter again would have made all the difference. It would have been a wonderful excuse.

Then, suddenly, she saw it. The whole plan in all its perfection flashed instantaneously before her inner eye.

'Oh!' she cried at the top of her voice, and ran into the kitchen where Mrs.

Roach was at the sink washing curtains. She waved the blue air letter excitedly. 'Oh, Roachy!' she said. 'Only think! She's coming home! Jonquil's coming home! Isn't it wonderful? She must be actually on her way now,' she said, pretending to consult the letter. 'They arrive on the third of March, she says.'

'Well, isn't that lovely,' said Mrs. Roach, without noticeable enthusiasm.

'It's nearly five years since I've seen her, did I tell you?'

'Yes, I know, dear. No wonder you're excited.'

'I think I'll do up her room, as a surprise; though there's not much time for that, is there? Still, bedspread and curtains . . . I shall turn your room into a dressing room for Guy,' she rattled on. 'You *must* come and see us while Jonquil's here. I should love you to meet her,' she gushed. Was it her fancy or had Mrs. Roach turned pale?

'You want me to leave, then?' Mrs. Roach murmured almost inaudibly.

'There really wouldn't be room for us all otherwise. I naturally do want them to feel absolutely at home.'

'Oh, of course. I do understand. But
. . . couldn't I just creep into the little
room over the bathroom, where I
wouldn't be in the way and they'd hardly
notice me, Mrs. Rampage dear?'

'I'm afraid that wouldn't do,' said Mrs.
Rampage firmly. 'I should hate them to
feel their stay was inconvenient in any
way. It would make them dreadfully
uncomfortable to think you had had to
turn out of your room for them.'

'Are they to be here long, then?'

'I sincerely hope so, after all these
years,' she said, with an impatient laugh.
(Really, the woman was too obtuse,
standing there as if she was going to cry!)

'Won't that be rather a lot of work for
you, Mrs. Rampage dear? If I was here to
take some of it off your shoulders — '

'I shall adore every minute of it. You
can't think how I long to have her all to
myself again; just my little family, and no
one else.'

'Ah, yes,' said the companion, in faintest reproach, 'when one has no longer a
family of one's own, one tends to forget

the peculiar sacredness of its ties.'

'Well, I mean, we just want to be together without any outsiders. If you don't mind my saying so.'

'Of course I don't mind. I should be a funny kind of person if I couldn't rejoice with you in your happiness because of my own anxieties. That would not be *me* at all. No, I shouldn't dream of darkening your little hour with my troubles. I shall begin looking for somewhere to go right away. You're not to bother your head about me one bit. I shall be all right. You did say they weren't coming till the third, didn't you? Might I — if the worse comes to the worst — stay here till then?'

'I couldn't let you stay quite till the third, Roachy, because of getting the room straight.'

'No, no. I only meant, if there is any difficulty in my finding somewhere to lay my poor tired head, might I just continue to stay on here for a week or two while I'm looking? Or must I leave at once? I'll do whatever you say, of course. I don't want to be a nuisance. Really, it's Winky Woo who's the problem. It matters so little to me what becomes of myself, but one can hardly walk the Embankment with a cat,' she said, with a bravely humorous little smile.

Mrs. Rampage weakly said that would be all right. And Mrs. Roach, as if to demonstrate her good intentions, went out the same day and bought a copy of *The Lady*, which she studied with an almost ostentatious conscientiousness, later sending off a number of letters.

Mrs. Rampage wondered, half-amused at her own dread, what would happen if Mrs. Roach had not found anywhere to go by the third. And she had deliberately chosen the third as being far enough off to give the roach time to find somewhere to go, and near enough to express a certain sense of immediacy. They watched one another like cat and mouse, each suspecting the other of bluff. Mrs. Roach did not quite believe in Jonquil's letter; and when Mrs. Rampage forgot all about the new bedspread and curtains she had spoken of for Jonquil's room, she was convinced that Mrs. Rampage was tricking her. And Mrs. Rampage equally doubted the earnestness and sincerity of Mrs. Roach's endeavours to find herself another home.

'It's too absurd!' Mrs. Rampage said to Etta, laughing through her fingers. 'How on earth am I to get rid of her? I thought if you told someone to go, in plain language, they usually took the hint. Not she, the old devil! I believe she means to stay forever.' Mrs. Rampage looked appalled as this new and horrifying thought occurred to her.

'I shouldn't be a bit surprised,' Henrietta said, with maddening nonchalance, squinting into the mirror as she rubbed peroxide into her parting. 'That woman strikes me as a bad lot, if you want to know, Luna. I took against her from the first, with her crafty little ways. I'd never have let her set foot in my house.'

'Thanks very much! This is a nice time to tell me, when it was you who encouraged me to take her in the first place, saying I could always get rid of her if I didn't like her. Shows how much you knew!'

'All right, ducky, don't go off the deep end! That was before I'd seen her. I couldn't know what a bloody bore she'd turn out to be.' Henrietta pushed up a swag of hair and looked at herself cruelly a moment. Then she pinched up the skin on her temples and, posing at herself in the glass, mused, 'I should look twenty years younger if I had my face lifted.'

'But you wouldn't *be* twenty years younger,' Luna said impatiently. 'How am I to get rid of her? Advise me, toad!'

'Treat her rough!'

'How do you mean?'

'You're too good to her, ducky, I told you before; you've made her thoroughly comfortable. The woman's not a fool, she knows when she's well off.' Henrietta corked up the peroxide and put the bottle back on the shelf. 'For instance, stop providing food for her. That'll shake her!'

Yes, Henrietta was right. Looking back, her generosity and her folly astounded her. Feeding the woman, treating her like a *queen:* what a mistake!

In the night an inspiration woke Mrs. Rampage: she would get rid of Lily! A pity to lose a good worker, of course, but it would be a clever discard if it meant losing Mrs. Roach as well. Surely that would prove just the little bit too much for the roach when she found herself expected to scrub out the stone kitchen, drag in the coals, and polish floors, brass, and silver till her arms dropped off. That, and suddenly finding herself unprovided with food, ought to do for her. Mrs. Rampage turned over and closed her eyes, seeing the roach on her hands and knees, rubbing . . . getting smaller as she advanced over the enormous floor, black as a beetle . . .

With the terrible meekness of despair, Lily said nothing when Mrs. Rampage told her. In silence she went on with her work, wringing out the cloth with hands as scarlet as rubber gloves.

Mrs. Roach saw immediately that something was wrong as soon as she entered the kitchen.

'What's the matter, dear?'

But Lily could not speak. She stood there obstinately, her upper lip drawn stiffly down over the words and tears that threatened to overflow.

'She's give me my cards,' she said at length.

'Oh, my dear! But why? What have you done?'

'She says she can't afford me. It wasn't anything I done, she was bound to admit that.'

'I'm sure I don't know how she thinks she'll manage without you.'

'All this big house to do in only six hours a week . . . it isn't human . . . And everlasting finding fault . . . I could tell her, there are some . . . ' Lily mumbled, holding up the wrung-out cloth for a screen between her and Mrs. Roach so that she should not see the tears of bitterness which had sprung so sharply into her eyes. At the end of her morning's work, Miss Graveyard simply pulled on her old felt and the coat with the rabbit-fur collar that was worn to leather, and went away, her cherry nose poking between her cowslip cheeks.

Peacock had gone, and now the daily woman had gone, and there was no one to bring a fresh atmosphere into the house for a few hours; no one to come between the two women and give them something other than themselves and their strange little war to think about.

It was worse, much worse, now that the two women were perpetually alone together. And even Mrs. Roach's remarkable placidity had an almost sour quality in it sometimes that was far from pleasant. She did not in the least mind being obliged to do her own cooking. Indeed, she preferred it — liking the simplest of foods. (One day she would give herself a little dab, wholesomely steamed in milk, with perhaps an egg custard baked in a brown dish to follow; and another it might be a cod steak in parsley sauce, and afterward a little semolina. There was nothing like good plain English cooking.)

('Nothing, thank God!' said Mrs. Rampage.)

For Mrs. Rampage had declared that she simply was not strong enough to do 'all that cooking' now that there was so much more to be done in the house. Though the fact was that she did less than ever, and sat around half the morning reading the paper; and most of the afternoon — if she was not going junking — she slept. Really, if Mrs. Roach had not done her best to keep the place reasonably clean, she shuddered to think of the filth that would have accumulated. Well, Mrs. Roach accepted that. Old ladies — as she had so often had occasion to remark before — had their funny little ways. But what absolutely amazed — yes, amazed and disgusted — her, was that when she showed Mrs. Rampage her account for these little items of food, Mrs. Rampage flatly declined to pay. 'Oh, no,' she said, 'if you can't eat the food provided . . . ' Completely overlooking the fact that she no longer provided any.

Mrs. Roach did not argue the point with her; she was too much of a lady. It was not a very nice thing to have to write to Mrs. Getaway about, but she knew *she* would make it right. 'Poor, dear Mrs. Rampage . . . '

The house was much less comfortable already, but both women secretly believed that could not last much longer. The lie about Jonquil's visit was exhausted. She had routed Mrs. Rampage there, and the recollection always brought out her prim smile.

'Damn that dirty lazy slut,' Mrs. Rampage, wiping the dust from a chair back, would say loud enough for the other to hear.

And Mrs. Roach would pause in the doorway to say cheerily, 'Talking to yourself again, dear? That's a bad sign.'

Now she was no longer so conscientiously sweet and patient with Mrs. Rampage's tiresome little ways. Now when Mrs. Rampage complained that something was missing, she dared to answer boldly: 'Do you think by any chance that I've taken it?'

Mrs. Rampage shrugged, slamming things about with her restless, irresponsible hands.

'How should I know?'

'My dear,' said Mrs. Roach, 'I pity you truly, with a nature like yours!'

It had got to the point where each thought only of how to annoy the other. Mrs. Rampage was much cleverer at this than Mrs. Roach; but Mrs. Roach was much less easily agitated than Mrs. Rampage, so that it worked out roughly the same in effect.

Mrs. Rampage would go out of the room, turning off the light as she went and leaving Mrs. Roach sewing in the dark. One point to Mrs. Rampage.

But Mrs. Roach waited until Mrs. Rampage was upstairs and then turned it on and would sit there comfortably, toasting her toes, till ten or eleven or *later*, while Mrs. Rampage in bed fretted with impatience, and would run out two or three times onto the landing in a perfect stew to bawl over the stairs, 'Aren't you ever going to bed, Mrs. Roach?'

'Presently, dear,' Mrs. Roach would flute back. And then it was Mrs. Rampage who suffered, thinking of the coal that was being burned, the electricity that was being wasted.

All day long in that tall quiet house the cat and the mouse watched each other, and hid from each other, and schemed.

* * *

Easter Monday, Mrs. Roach went down to Edenbridge for the day. She badly needed a breath of fresh air. Eleanor was quite shocked at the sight of her.

'My poor darling, what have they been doing to you? You look worn out.'

'It has been rather trying,' Mrs. Roach confessed. 'But you will cheer me up and put new life into me; you always do.'

It was a day of glorious sunshine, one of those rare treasured days as hot as summer, and they took their lunch out under the apple tree, wheeling the old man carefully across the grass. He sat like Oedipus at Colonus, feeling the shadows and sunlight moving on his skin, hearing the birds. The meal was passed restfully without much talk. Afterward Eleanor took him back to the house for his nap and then rejoined Norah beneath the tree, where they watched milky clouds form and dissolve high up in the blue.

'The peace!' Mrs. Roach murmured. 'The heavenly peace!'

Eleanor clasped her hands behind her head and said nothing for quite a while, trying to think how best to say what had to be said. And, as is so often the way when one thinks heavily round a delicate subject, the more one thinks, the more the words blurt themselves out in the end.

'I wish you'd leave there, Norah,' Eleanor said, clumsy with nervousness.

'Ah, don't I wish I could, too!' Mrs. Roach said, closing her eyes and tipping her face to the sunlight.

'You'll probably tell me to mind my own business, but I can't bear to see you looking so ill. You look worse now than when you first went there.'

'Nonsense, Nell,' Mrs. Roach said drowsily.

'Dearest, it isn't nonsense. I worry so about you. That beastly old woman is *killing* you.'

'I'm simply a bit tired. It's the time of year. I expect I need a holiday.'

'Why don't you take one?' she dared enquire.

Mrs. Roach opened one blue eye, quizzical, astonished.

'What's all this? How can I take a holiday? Don't be absurd, my dear.'

'You're not to be angry and say I'm being insulting, Norah darling, please.' In her agitation Eleanor knelt upright beside her. 'Look, all these months I've been saving — not from Father, I promise — I've been knitting, gloves and things, for people . . . I've made nearly nine pounds — '

'And you'd give it all to me,' Mrs. Roach said, sitting up and embracing her tenderly. 'You make me want to cry,' said Mrs. Roach. And just for a moment they did weep in one another's arms. 'Fancy crying on a lovely day like this,' Mrs. Roach said, blowing her nose.

'You could take a little holiday with it,' Eleanor said eagerly.

'My dear, it's no use. I can't. Don't let's talk any more about it.'

'But I want to talk about it, Norah.'

'I say no. Don't be obstinate and naughty.'

'I'm going to be obstinate and naughty, though. Just for this once. What sort of a friend would I be to pass it over in silence? You can't go on like this. You're not happy there, and it's too much for you.' Mrs. Roach did not respond. 'Why does it make you angry when I say that? I can see you're angry by the way you're digging your fingers into the grass. What I can't understand is why you don't want to leave. You're always saying how tiresome she is. Why stay?'

'I can manage her.'

'But why stay?' Eleanor insisted.

'Because . . . ' Mrs. Roach said lightly.

'Because what?'

'Oh, Eleanor, what deadly persistence! All right. I must stay because I promised I would.'

'Promised? Who did you promise?'

'Mrs. Getaway. She's gone to South Africa, and I promised her I'd stick.'

'May one ask what she has to do with it?'

'Only that she happens to be my old lady's niece, and she got me the job, and I should hate to let her down. Also,' Mrs. Roach went on after a minute, in a light, punishing voice, 'difficult though she may be at times, I happen to be rather fond of my old lady, and I've an idea — presumptuous and absurd though it may seem to you — that she doesn't altogether dislike me.'

'Ah, now we're getting at the truth!' Eleanor said with a cruel laugh, scrambling to her feet. 'I thought we should eventually.'

'You've asked for it often enough.'

'Yes, I'd rather have the truth however much it hurts. You don't want to leave, do you?' she said accusingly.

'I hoped I had more or less conveyed that notion.'

'Yes, unmistakably.' Eleanor pressed the back of her hand against her teeth and stared up blindly at the blue mosaic of sky and boughs. 'But why?' she said huskily. 'I think our . . . friendship has given me the right to ask why.'

'If I had thought you would understand, I would have told you before,' Mrs. Roach said coldly.

'Oh! Then it's something you're ashamed of?'

'No, why should I be ashamed because my old lady has tried to repay me for a little of my kindness?'

'What exactly does that mean?'

'It means exactly this: she is leaving me her house and furniture — some of the furniture — providing, of course, I stay with her.'

'Oh, I understand!' said Eleanor, going off into a fit of laughter. 'God, how I understand! Fancy you thinking I wouldn't. It was what I said would happen all along: you'd stay with her forever.' Her words came out jagged. 'Naturally you couldn't think of leaving her if she has promised you all those things to stay. I can quite see that all our little plans come nowhere, mean nothing, compared with that,' she ended, with a sound that was more like a sob than a laugh.

'May I never have any possessions again? Must I remain a pauper to the end of my days, dependent on your charity? Is that what you wish for me?'

'You never spoke of it as charity before,' Eleanor said, in a low voice hardly to be heard. 'I didn't know you thought of it like that. It was you who suggested in the first place that we should live together. Why did you say it, if you felt like that about it?' Her heart was beating so heavily it made her afraid.

'Put yourself in my place and ask yourself how you would like it, after what I've been accustomed to,' Mrs. Roach said bitterly. 'Do you think I find it pleasant to be without a penny and to have no home — nothing? I don't complain, so perhaps it has never occurred to you before that my position is not attractive; let it occur to you now.'

'No, I had no idea,' said Eleanor, leaning back against the tree and shutting her eyes. 'You always said how glad you were that you had no possessions to worry about getting motheaten or rusted or stolen. You used to say it was easier to fly up to heaven without pennies in your pocket to weigh you down.'

'Oh, God!' exclaimed Mrs. Roach, dropping her forehead into her hand. 'Have I to account for every careless word I uttered?'

'How else can I judge?' Eleanor said huskily.

'Well, I was mistaken too. I see now what your friendship means. It isn't *me* at all that you are fond of; it's what I give you. You haven't a thought for *me*. I'm to go drudging on, waiting for you to be free — this year, next year, sometime, never!' cried Mrs. Roach, stung.

'Is it my fault that I'm not free? What do you expect me to do? *Kill* the old man?'

The row went nagging bitterly on till Mr. Fielding woke from his snooze just before tea and dragged the women back into the world of Things and Time. The quarrel could not be carried any further, and Mrs. Roach left at once, without tea and without making it up with Eleanor — nobody could forgive all at once the things they had said to one another. Besides, Eleanor must be punished. Punished also for ruining Mrs. Roach's day out. There was no hope of salvaging the rest of it, though the sun was still as bright and the birds still sang as loud. It was to 'blow away the cobwebs', to 'sweep some of the bitterness out of her soul' that Mrs. Roach went striding over the hills.

Even the nicest people liked you to feel you were in their power. And if one had not the means for independence, the slightest sign of weakness was fatal. It meant one must be always on guard. As now. Eleanor took advantage, Eleanor presumed. Eleanor must come and beg her pardon; Eleanor must be made to feel how precarious her hold was on her friend. Favour and financial dependence must be glossed over as insignificant, compared with the wayward spirit blowing where it listeth and ever alert to the slightest hint of insult or injustice.

But it was a tiresome road to travel, and not to be compared with real independence. 'Who can blame me for wanting to be independent?' Mrs. Roach moaned to the wind. Besides, it was true what she told Eleanor; it might be years yet before the old man died, and Mrs. Roach was no longer so young. She yearned for a place of her own. And now at last she had a hope to cling to, if she played her cards well (horrible phrase!). Not that she was so foolish or self-deceiving as to imagine that Mrs. Rampage would really leave her anything — the old lady was too selfish for that, she knew. Besides, when there was Family, it was not to be expected. She was too wise to permit herself to feel injured over that. That was not her way. That was not what she was after. The success of her plan depended on making herself indispensable to the old lady. And really — though she said it herself — who could have been sweeter or more patient than she? The time would come when the poor old thing would not be fit to live alone, would not be able to manage, and then 'Roachy' would be there to take things into her capable hands and look after her. All those little odds and ends lying about uselessly which Mrs. Rampage said were worth so much — it wasn't right or fair! What good were they? And who would miss them? Only a foolish, and failing old woman whose word no one would believe. The doctor had been prepared for this, and so had Mrs. Getaway. Why should she now be deprived of her reward for all these months of work and patient planning because of a foolish jealous girl? Half a dozen of those trifles would keep her for years. And she could do so *much* good with the money. *Then* she could go to Eleanor and not be empty-handed. *Then* she could leave her whenever she chose; and the threat of that would be enough to keep Eleanor amenable. Or she could live alone; and that might be best of all. In any case, she was in the right of the quarrel. She would be mad to leave just because Eleanor was jealous and wanted her to; and then nowhere to go again and all that anxiety. Moreover, even if the old man died tomorrow, who could tell whether there would be enough money left to live on?

Mrs. Roach's argument had soothed her feelings wonderfully and she stopped at a wayside farmhouse to make a hearty tea. Her walk had given her an appetite and cleared her head. She bought three brown eggs to take back with her, a present for Mrs. Rampage.

★   ★   ★

But Eleanor couldn't escape. Eleanor was obliged to sit with her father and try to say yes and no in the right places while the tears ran down her face and the wretched argument went running round and round in her head, in chunks, in sentences, repeating itself endlessly. By half-past five she was planning to run down the lane to the bus stop and see if she could catch one more word with Norah. Even the thought of it made her heart beat so wildly that she knew she would never do it: she hadn't the courage, she hadn't the strength. Norah, when she was angry, was too terrifying to face.

There would have been time to spare to make up the quarrel, if she had gone to the bus stop. For, because of the glorious holiday weather, the coaches were all so laden that Mrs. Roach had nearly an hour to wait by the roadside before one could pick her up. And then they crawled home in a string of traffic and were stuck twenty-five minutes at Leatherhead. It was half-past ten when they arrived at Victoria. By the time she reached home it was gone eleven. And then she couldn't get in. The doors were locked.

Mrs. Rampage must have presumed

she wasn't coming back that night, and so she had locked up (she never would go to bed without locking up everywhere). Mrs. Roach stood in the dark porch, ringing; she did hope there would not be a scene about this, there had been enough scenes for one day.

Something soft brushed her ankle and she bent down. 'Darling, you out too!' She lifted the cat onto her shoulder. 'Let's go and see if we can get in somewhere else; Mrs. R. must be asleep.'

She walked round the house, but all the downstairs windows were shuttered and could not be pried open because the shutters were inside the windows. 'Well, here's a how d'ye do,' she murmured into the cat's soft flank, and pressed her thumb on the bell again and held it there. Well, what did Mrs. Rampage expect her to do? She could hardly stay out all night. Though, God knew, she was tired enough to sleep against the wall. Her shoulders slumped with weariness. She was so 'down' she could have cried. St. Anne's struck the half-hour. There was not even a neighbour she dared knock up; everyone was abed and their houses in darkness.

Not until that actual moment did it enter Mrs. Roach's head that this was anything more than a dismal little mishap, to be laughed over wryly next day at breakfast. Her heart began to pound as it came over her that it was a deliberate, devilish attempt of the old girl's to turn her out. She must be off her head if she thought she would get away with *that*! The irony of it, on top of her quarrel with Eleanor, struck Mrs. Roach disagreeably; but indignation had lent her a spurious vitality and her steps rang like a soldier's on the empty pavement.

She told the police sergeant on night duty quite simply what had happened.

'My old lady's turned me out,' she said. 'I come back from my day out and find the door locked against me. What am I to do?'

She explained to them that she had not been given notice, not really, although she was aware that the old lady had taken a dislike to her. Old ladies did get fanciful at times. Her job was not to take any notice of the old lady's fads and fancies, but to look after her and keep her out of mischief on behalf of her family, now that she was no longer fit to be alone. The old lady had kept back her trunks.

Ladylike and persecuted though she was, it had all to be down in black and white, question and answer, before any steps could be taken.

The sergeant took a constable along with him. He didn't ring; he banged on the knocker thunderously.

'That ought to waken the dead!' Mrs. Roach laughed nervously.

It woke Mrs. Rampage, anyway. The light went on upstairs, and presently the landing window shot up and Mrs. Rampage leaned out in her sleeping cap to demand crossly who was making such a din.

The sergeant put up a finger to his hat.

'Might I speak to you a moment, madam?'

'What is it?'

'Could you come down, please?'

'No, I can't . . . In my night-things, and for all I know you might be going to murder me,' Mrs. Rampage said shrilly.

(Mrs. Roach looked at the policeman significantly.)

'I'm a police officer, madam.'

'I dare say. Well? What do you want?'

'I've a lady with me who says she lives here and has been locked out.'

'She did live here — out of the goodness of my heart. She doesn't live here anymore.'

'Oh, Mrs. Rampage, dear!'

'No, I've had enough. Anyone else would have turned you out years ago. Take my advice and clear out while you've got the chance. If you try to pester me, I warn you, I shall give you in charge.'

'Madam, the law does not permit — '

'Don't tell me what the law permits. I give that woman in charge as a nuisance; I can't get rid of her.'

'One moment, please!' The sergeant held up a hand in order to be heard, and at the same time windows began flying up in the neighbouring houses, for it was long past midnight, and other voices were added to the hubbub.

'What's the row?'

'What's happening?'

'It's the party at No. 5, carrying on about something,' someone said.)

'A little quiet down there, if you please. People are trying to sleep,' a man called to them angrily.

'I won't be bullyragged! What's this country coming to?' Mrs. Rampage slammed down the window.

'Well, what now?' said Mrs. Roach despondently.

The constable had his thumb on the bell. They could hear it ringing away inside.

Mrs. Rampage came thumping down in the darkness, weeping.

' . . . an old woman! Am I to have no peace?' she said angrily. 'I thought the police were supposed to protect people — '

('Exactly so, madam,' murmured the sergeant.)

'No, I won't let her in; you can't make me!'

'Madam, the law does not permit — ' the sergeant essayed again patiently.

'I shall complain to your superintendent. I shall take your number. Forcing your way in here and daring to — '

('Better slip in, miss, if you can.')

'Now, dear,' Mrs. Roach began.

'Don't you touch me!' the other screamed hysterically. 'You wicked woman!'

'Oh, what a bad girl, with no slippers on! Do you want to get your death of cold? And I've bought you a little present from the country,' Mrs. Roach said, leading her away without a backward glance.

She could not help smiling quietly to herself. Even her disadvantages she turned to account. Now the police, too, knew that Mrs. Rampage was peculiar.

7

Mrs. Rampage scarcely slept that night, she was so angry and humiliated by the scandal Mrs. Roach had caused. She walked up and down, up and down her bedroom, catching her heels in the hem of her silk wrap with small rending sounds and biting her fingers, while she tried to think of some way of getting rid of the roach. She felt cold and rather ill and shaken, and from time to time she took little swallows of neat brandy from her late husband's old silver flask, mopping up the silly tears that kept gliding down her face without warning. To divert her troubled mind she invented outrageous, impossible, and useless schemes for disposing of 'that bitch, that devil'.

Presently, she climbed into bed, and lay back on the pillows watching the shadows move on the ceiling; but they kept forming into images of the roach; so she sat up again and turned on the light and wrote a ten-page letter to Cissie, blotted with tears and full of wandering unfinished sentences (because of the brandy) and a great many obscure allusions to past quarrels with Cissie's long-dead mother, 'who had always been in the wrong, like Cissie'. Old memories came back to her, scaldingly alive ('You've made my life *hell*, you and your mother, with your interference — and when Charles was alive he knew all about it and often said — that time when your poor father wanted to come and stay and she said no — because she could not bear, though God knows I had done *nothing* — taking her in as I did out of the goodness of my heart, and the end of it is, she is *killing* me with the worry of it . . . ').

'That was a good letter,' she thought. It seemed to her that she had said everything in it that was necessary. And afterwards she fell into an easy doze and dreamed a little plot which still seemed feasible when she woke. Concerned with these thoughts, the calamity of the ruined sheet spattered with ink — where the pen had rolled from her fingers as she slept — did not cause her to wail aloud her vexation at the malice of Things, as she would otherwise have done.

She just went about her business the next day with a quiet, rather frightening smile on her pallid face. Mrs. Roach discreetly did not speak either.

She watched her guardedly from the corner of her eye, wondering what the next move was to be. Mrs. Roach was afraid. It had been an unpleasantly near thing last night. She could see herself hardly daring to venture outside the house for fear of being shut out again. But that was absurd. Such a situation could not endure for long. 'Oh, she'll come round,' she told herself reassuringly. 'Given time, I'll get round her again.'

As a sort of penance, or an omen of future good behavior, Mrs. Roach went down on her knees meekly and washed over the kitchen floor, which had not been touched since Lily went and had already a thin coating of grime patterned with grease.

Rather surprisingly, Mrs. Rampage

called loudly down the stairs, 'I'm just going out to post a letter.' But Mrs. Roach, absorbed in her worries, did not pay much attention to the unusualness of this. Or perhaps, with that fraction of her mind that noticed it, she thought of it as the first sign of the old girl coming round. The old girl was always the one to apologize and bustle round guiltily making it up.

Mrs. Rampage was gone for scarcely longer than it would have taken her to post a letter, and when she returned she was accompanied by a workman — a long, thin man, like a grasshopper in a white apron, who leaped up the stairs three at a time.

Mrs. Rampage left him at work and tiptoed down to see what Mrs. Roach was doing, to prevent her, if necessary, from going upstairs.

The pail stood in the middle of the half-washed floor, and Mrs. Roach was sitting on a hard kitchen chair, stuffing herself with malted milk out of a jar as eagerly as if she were a heart sufferer inhaling amyl nitrate.

When she saw Mrs. Rampage watching her she felt as guilty as a greedy schoolgirl; she *had* to explain . . . the sudden exertion . . . she was obliged to pump sugar into her bloodstream immediately or she would have fainted from sheer exhaustion.

Mrs. Rampage was elaborately uninterested, humming a busy little tune. Neither of them saw the locksmith till he coughed politely.

'All present and correct, madam,' he said gaily, like an actor. 'I left the key in the door; and I don't anticipate you'll have any more trouble.'

Mrs. Rampage hustled him out before he could say more, and ran upstairs. The door to Mrs. Roach's room stood open.

Mrs. Rampage cried out, '*Oh! . . . Oh!*' in a shocked voice.

The blood rushed dark red into her face. She stared, incredulous.

Wherever her eye fell, there was one of her most treasured possessions. Some of them she had not seen for so long she had forgotten she owned them. Or had supposed them safe in the boxroom.

Her beautiful red Persian rag, for instance, that ought to be in the boxroom sewn up in its hessian with paradichlorobenzene, instead lay on the floor, messed with cat hair.

The wicker chair, the art silk spread and the Indian cotton mat were there no longer. On the bed now was a length of fine old crimson brocade she had picked up years ago and intended to have mounted as a bedspread one day, that Mrs. Roach must have filched from one of the trunks. The wicker chair with its frayed edges had been supplanted by a little Chippendale bedroom chair that only needed re-covering.

Her electric kettle that she always kept as polished as a pin now stood tarnishing on the hearth, and beside it an Irish wool lap rug — that Mrs. Rampage had turned out the boxroom in her search for only the other day — scrunched into a nest in which Winky Woo lay curled up fast asleep.

On the table, actually on the very piece of Carrickmacross Mrs. Rampage had given her, a handful of anemones lolled in one of Mrs. Rampage's best Waterford glasses.

And on the dressing table, next to the heart-shaped Sheraton looking-glass on a stand that the woman had taken from the guest room without a word, there stood the adorable little Dresden pintray held aloft by a cherub which belonged to Mrs. Rampage's own dressing table, and whose loss the woman must have heard Mrs. Rampage bewailing like an Egyptian mourner.

At this point Mrs. Rampage recognized that these things must have been taken deliberately, and she felt sick, as one always does before a big fight. Sick, but triumphant. This time she'd got her.

If she had not been in such a state of excitement she might not have attacked so boldly. Directly she looked up and saw Mrs. Roach standing in the doorway, she cried out, '*Thief!*'

Mrs. Roach could feel her neck redden, but the expression on her face remained as imperturbable as ever. 'I shall keep perfectly calm, whatever she says,' she was telling herself over and over, to still the agitated beating of her heart. She clasped her hands together in a way that a spiritualist once had told her cut off aggressive or harmful influences.

She said: 'I *beg* your pardon! I hardly think I can have heard you correctly.'

'You're a dirty thief! A liar and a thief,' Mrs. Rampage said loudly, trembling with excitement.

'I'm sure you mean to be insulting,' Mrs. Roach said carefully, 'but I'm afraid I've not the least idea what you're talking about.'

'You know bloody well what I'm talking about, you wicked woman. Don't pretend!' snapped Mrs. Rampage like an angry little French bulldog. 'You've been going over my trunks and sneaking things out of my rooms and hiding them up here. No wonder you were so careful to keep your door locked!'

Mrs. Roach opened her true blue eyes, as if offering to Mrs. Rampage all their innocence and sincerity; and the idea in all its beautiful simplicity came into her head there and then.

'But, my dear Mrs. Rampage,' she said,

'this is simply one of your delusions. Of course I haven't taken anything of yours. As if I would, my dear!'

What a brazen liar the woman was.

'Really? Then what about *this* that you took off my very dressing table?' Mrs. Rampage said, holding up the little Dresden pintray in a shaking hand.

A look of perfect consternation came over Mrs. Roach's face.

'But, Mrs. Rampage! Dear, you gave me that!'

Mrs. Rampage stared.

'I *gave* it to you? You're potty! Why, that belonged to my mother; what on earth should I have given it to you for?' she said, in her rudest voice.

Mrs. Roach closed her eyes in pain.

'This is terribly distressing,' she murmured. 'You can't have forgotten. You gave it to me for my birthday, last month.'

'Of course I didn't! You're a pathological liar, that's what you are.' She began to understand the situation. 'I suppose you thought I'd never find out; and now that — to your dismay — I have, you're trying to lie your way out of it by pretending you're entitled to the things. But I'm afraid that won't wash, madam.' She laughed; but the patient look on the roach's face, so convincedly righteous, gave Mrs. Rampage a twitch of doubt: could she have made a mistake? Have given her the pintray and then forgotten it? To still her qualms, she picked up the Waterford glass into which Mrs. Roach had stuck some anemones and said scornfully, 'I suppose I gave you this too.'

She saw Mrs. Roach look at her oddly.

'Why, no; of course not. That's mine.'

'My God, you've got a nerve! Regardless of the fact that this happens to be one of a set and the other five are in the glass cabinet downstairs,' Mrs. Rampage said indignantly, clutching the piece to her with her free hand.

'Yours weren't the only ones made in that pattern,' Mrs. Roach explained easily, with a smile of pity for the silly old thing. 'I'm sure I've mentioned often enough that I had one similar to yours.'

'Then, do tell me where you bought it, because I'd love to get some more like that.'

But Mrs. Roach ignored the sarcasm, and answered quietly and seriously, 'I've always had it. It's been in the family for years. One of the few good pieces left to me, alas.'

'How interesting!' Mrs. Rampage said briskly, marching from the room with the glass in one hand and the Dresden piece in the other.

Mrs. Roach said, 'Oh, forgive me!' and put out a hand to stop her.

Exactly what happened then, it is hard to say. Mrs. Roach declared that Mrs. Rampage let it slip as she tried to pull it away. Mrs. Rampage, on the other hand, swore that the roach had deliberately knocked it out of her grasp — deliberately, so that it shouldn't be compared with the rest of the set. Whoever was to blame, for a moment the two women did a kind of staggering dance step together, the water rose up suddenly and hung poised in the air in a glassy mass — and then it collapsed in a shower on to the sleeve of Mrs. Rampage's green jersey, and the wine glass exploded into shivers of light.

Mrs. Rampage burst into tears. She hit the roach smack in the face, with fury.

It was Mrs. Roach's turn to cry out then. She put a hand to her nose to feel if it was bleeding (it certainly felt as if it was; it was agony!). There is nothing like a smart blow on the nose for making the saintliest of us lose our temper.

'*Hitting* people!' said Mrs. Roach, with one hand to where it throbbed between her eyes. 'I could have you up for assault.'

'You did it on purpose, you bloody swine!' Mrs. Rampage sobbed. 'That was my best set! They cost twenty pounds.'

'You might have broken my nose.'

'I wish to God I had,' said Mrs. Rampage, going down on her knees as one mourns at the grave of a loved one.

'One would think at your age one would have a little more self-control. Working yourself up over a piece of glass!' Mrs. Roach said, the hatred coming out with her anger.

''A piece of glass', you call it, you ignorant fool! The value of that 'piece of glass' was its beauty and its antiquity and the craftsmanship that went to make it.

Oh, I could murder you! If it had been yours — '

'It *was* mine. I told you that. Just because I don't allow myself to become hysterical over my possessions, few though they are and the more precious to me for that very reason . . . And then to lose your temper over a mere accident, and cry and carry on and strike people; I've never *heard* of anyone going on like that.'

Mrs. Rampage, on her knees gathering up the fragments, murmured incredulously, 'All these months I've had you here at my expense, and this is how you repay me, by trying to steal my things. No one would believe it!'

'I'm afraid no one would,' Mrs. Roach agreed.

'You'd better pack up your things and go — before I send for the police,' Mrs. Rampage said, tart at the insolence of this last remark.

'Oh, the poor police! Are they to be dragged into it again? After last night? They didn't take much notice of you then, did they?' Mrs. Roach laughed.

'I've an idea they'll regard a matter of theft rather more seriously,' Mrs. Rampage said, flushing angrily at the woman's gall.

'Ah, you think so? I think they'll simply look on it as yet another spiteful attack on the part of a *crazy old woman*.'

It occurred to Mrs. Rampage disagreeably that the roach might be a little mad. She said, as cheerfully as possible, 'You may be right.' And looked away. And pounced suddenly at the chimney piece: behind the china lamb with the cross on its back, she had caught sight of the corner of a leather box. It was the box of seals Cissie had given her.

'Are you going to pretend I gave you this? Or are you going to pretend it's your own?' she cried in triumph. Something like this was just what she needed! She opened it quickly to see if they were all there. 'And you said you'd never seen them! My God, what a liar!'

'I never have seen it before,' said Mrs. Roach, quite quietly. 'You must have put it there yourself. I suppose you meant it for a trap. Only I didn't happen to fall into it.'

'No, you've had your chance,' Mrs. Rampage said indignantly. (The woman had an answer for everything!) 'I shan't argue with you anymore. It's no use. I shall go straight to the police.' She picked up the seals and the pintray and stumped to the door.

Mrs. Roach waited in silence while the other woman tried to open the door with her hands full. Then she said, in quite an ordinary voice, not at all as if she was in a raging temper: 'I think I should warn you that the police know about you. Which makes it extremely improbable that they would credit anything you say.'

Mrs. Rampage asked her indifferently what she meant, as she tucked the little box under her chin and opened the door with her free hand.

'They know why I'm here. They know why I *have* to stay on here, even though you keep telling me to go and trying to get rid of me. Because if I wasn't here to look after you, *you'd be put away*.'

Mrs. Rampage turned white as a rag.

'What are you talking about?' she said, in a voice that came out horribly squeaky.

'Everybody knows about you,' Mrs. Roach said, with a terrible smile. (Two could play at this game!) 'Ask anyone. All this forgetting, all these delusions, are symptoms. Oh, yes, the doctor warned me (that time after you had that little stroke, which we told you was the flu), he warned me then that it would get worse and worse, and you would need someone to be responsible for you. 'She's not fit to live alone' were his very words, and that was why Mrs. Getaway begged me to stay.'

Mrs. Rampage tried to speak but no sound came. Her legs were both wobbly and immovable as stones. 'I'll send for Jonquil . . . I'll tell Henrietta!' she thought desperately. 'Someone must help me!'

'You ought to be so grateful to me,' Mrs. Roach said cruelly, 'for not letting your daughter put you in a home.'

These words, even without the malice which envenomed them, so shocked Mrs. Rampage that she only wanted to shut her ears to them, to get away, quickly, anywhere.

' . . . forgetting the time . . . dinner . . . ' she mumbled, as an excuse. And somehow she got down the stairs on her shaking old legs. She couldn't stay in the house with that woman a moment longer, she was too afraid, and she ran out into the icy street just as she was. She was so shocked that all her wits were scattered and she hardly knew where she was going or why. Presently she found herself among the shops, and to prove to herself that she was perfectly normal she impetuously entered the first one she came to.

But once there she could not for the life of her think what she wanted. She stood there blankly with her eyes staring and her mouth open. An odd figure, without a hat or coat on in this biting wind, and all her hair dishevelled. She saw the grocer look at her quite anxiously when he asked her if she was wanting anything.

'I do want something,' she said, trying to pull herself together, ' . . . but I've forgotten,' she was going to say, but clapped her hand to her mouth with a wild look of horror, for 'forgetting' was one of the words the woman had threatened her with.

Two young girls in white aprons at the other end of the counter were whispering together and trying to suppress their giggles as they eyed her.

The grocer was reeling out a formidable list of suggestions . . .

' . . . tea, coffee, cocoa, condiments, salad cream, salt, vinegar, floor polish, biscuits, cheese — nice consignment just come in of blue cheese, madam — tinned apricots, tinned pears, golden syrup, porridge, cereals — '

'Cereal,' said Mrs. Rampage, hooking on to a word as it slipped past.

The grocer made a sign, and one of the giggling girls came forward to serve her.

With a great effort of concentration, she thought of one or two other things she needed. The girl looked positively half-witted with the effort she was making not to laugh (she did not dare to catch Reenie's eye).

'Five and fourpence halfpenny,' she said, touching the packets with her pencil as she added them up.

But Mrs. Rampage hadn't got five and fourpence halfpenny. She hadn't any money on her at all; all she had with her was an antique leather case of seals in one hand and a china ornament in the other.

She stammered, 'I haven't any money.' She stared round the shop: it seemed to her that everyone was looking at her. 'I was in such a hurry,' she said loudly, so that all should hear and understand. 'Never mind. I'll come back.'

The girl was biting her lip hard and sucking in her cheeks; her eyes were downcast and her whole body quivered. Mrs. Rampage could see she was laughing helplessly at her, as cruel children do laugh at old people not quite right in the head that they see talking and nodding to themselves. It became apparent to Mrs. Rampage with a stab of fear that people were regarding her — just as Mrs. Roach said they did. She could not bear all those eyes watching from under their lids. She felt herself surrounded by enemies. She took two swaying steps as if she was balancing on a deck. She was visited suddenly by the hideous notion that Mrs. Roach was pursuing her, would burst into this shop and make an appalling scene about her. 'In this way people are driven into madness,' she thought.

The grocer came behind the girl and gave her a sharp dig in the back which quickly wiped the smile off her face.

'That will be quite all right, madam. We'll send the goods round for you,' he said. ('These girls!' he thought.)

Wherever she went, it seemed to Mrs. Rampage that she had never noticed people's eyes before. The butcher smiled when he said good morning, and for the first time she saw how sinister and insincere his smile was. She had the feeling that in all the shops they were watching her and passing on reports of her behavior. They were all in complicity. *In this way people are driven into madness*, she thought again in fear.

8

The thing to do, of course, was to go and see Geoffrey. He would advise her. As soon as this thought entered Mrs. Rampage's head, a couple of days after the big row, she felt much more cheerful. Yes, wonderfully brighter, but still so muddled with anger and fright that she forgot to ring up and make an appointment with Geoffrey's clerk. Forgetting this, she stampeded in: 'I want to see Mr. Bede.'

They were Kirtle, Bede & Son, but Kirtle and Bede were dead and only Son was left, and he was in his sixties. But he was clever, everyone said so, and Mrs. Rampage had known him for more than thirty years; he had been a friend of Charles.

The clerk said, Yes, and, Had she an appointment?

Mrs. Rampage said, 'No. But I've got to see him at once. It's important.'

187

The clerk looked nervous — he was very young — and slid out of the room. Old Mr. Deeks came in, very quavery. Hopeless! Geoff ought to send him away. Very courteously, very slowly, he fumbled for her name and bade her good morning and asked how he could be of assistance to her.

'Ah, Mr. Bede's engaged just at present, I fear. Very busy all day, yes.'

'I wouldn't keep him five minutes. You could winkle him out for me, couldn't you?' she said persuasively.

The old man sniggered, positively.

'Dear lady! I wouldn't dare!'

'You could make an excuse. I've got to see him.'

She did undoubtedly show signs of distress, in her ragged make-up, a wrinkled stocking and dirty nails, Mr. Deeks thought to himself.

'Luna! What is it?' Geoffrey said, not pleased.

'Oh, Geoff, such a nuisance! I hate to bother you, but I don't know how to get rid of the silly woman.'

'Look here, I can't see you now: I've a

client. Why on earth didn't you make an appointment?'

'I didn't want the woman to hear me ringing up; it might have put her on her guard,' she said quickly. 'But I won't keep you five minutes.'

Bede knew all about that!

He said, 'My dear, you'll just have to wait till I've finished. I would take you out to luncheon, but I already have a luncheon appointment. I can spare you five minutes before I leave.'

She was left to dangle her legs from the shallow bench and yawn in that fusty atmosphere till her jaws cracked and her eyes watered. She had almost forgotten what she wanted to say by the time Geoffrey was ready to see her.

'I've been trying to get rid of her for ages and she simply takes no notice,' she began eagerly.

'You'd better begin at the beginning, Luna. Who is this woman?'

'My dear, I've no idea! She *says* she's a Mrs. Roach. Cissie wished her onto me, God knows why. Oh, she'd been ill or something and had no money; with the result that she's stolen all my things — '

'Just a minute. When was this?'

'That she began stealing? From the time — '

'No. When did she come to you?'

'Last October. I remember exactly because it was just after my birthday and Cissie gave me a set of seals — '

'Never mind about that now, Luna. I'm trying to get the picture clear.'

'I was only going to tell you that she stole the seals too,' Mrs. Rampage said reproachfully.

'Very well, she came to you in October. What was the contract?'

'Contract? There was no *contract*.'

'What were the terms, then, if you prefer that? You must have agreed terms together. Come, now!'

'Well, I never dreamed she'd stay so long in the first place. I thought it was just till she got strong enough to take a proper job again. She'd been a warden in some ghastly hostel for old folks, till she broke down.'

'Did you take up her references?'

Mrs. Rampage stared.

'I never thought of it. I supposed she was a lady,' she said sourly.

'Wasn't that rather foolish?'

'Well, Cissie introduced her. I naturally thought she would have seen to all that.'

'Oh, God, Luna, how many times did Charles say to you, 'Never suppose that anyone has ever done anything'? Women!' he said, opening his hands in despair.

'I hope you're not going to be one of those bloody lawyers who always try to make out their own client is in the wrong,' she said crossly. 'I was only trying to do the woman a good turn. She didn't look like a crook . . . I suppose they never do,' she conceded gloomily.

It took much longer than five minutes before he even got the story straight in his head. And then of course the first thing he asked was, 'Why didn't you go to the police?'

Just what she didn't want to hear.

She said hurriedly, 'Geoffrey, how horrible! I couldn't do that. I should hate to drag the police into this.'

She was not going to speak of her brush with the police the night she had tried locking out the roach; better not mention it, men were funny and it might prejudice him. Nor did she intend Geoffrey to hear the real reason why she had not called in the police when she discovered her things in the roach's room; the roach had panicked her and she had lost her head, but still — better say nothing.

'I thought, Geoffrey, if you'd be an angel and come and speak to her yourself, you could put the fear of God into her and she really would clear out,' she said, with her spaniel look.

Bede had already been obliged to tell the clerk to ring through to Mr. Devereux and tell him not to wait for him, he would be late. And since the thing had to be done — for poor Charles's sake (Luna was a dead loss as a client anyway) — one might as well get done with it right away. A pity! Devereux had a nice taste in wines, and there was a little place off Fleet Street . . . He sighed; picked up his cane; took his hat. 'We'll get a sandwich and a Guinness at The Black Dog,' he said.

Mrs. Rampage opened the door without knocking, so that Mrs. Roach was disclosed sitting on the bed, stitching, and Bede saw her in that first moment unprepared. She looked startled but not discomposed. She was not what he expected. Without prejudging, he saw what Luna meant: she looked a lady.

Mrs. Rampage said roughly — a warning, not an introduction: 'This is my lawyer, Mrs. Roach.'

Mrs. Roach gave him a grave little bow.

Luna at once began excitedly pointing out to Geoffrey the things Mrs. Roach had taken.

'Are you quite sure you didn't put them in here yourself before Mrs. Roach came, Luna?'

'Don't be silly, Geoffrey! In a servant's bedroom!' she said impatiently, fingering the little Sheraton mirror.

'That happens to belong to me,' Mrs. Roach interpolated quietly.

'That's a lie!' Luna said excitedly. 'She says everything is hers, or else that I gave it to her. It's all lies!'

'You see, I have no home, Mr . . . oh, Bede! Won't you sit down, Mr. Bede? There's no need for us to be uncomfortable, is there?' (Mrs. Rampage sucked in her breath sharply at this impudent usurpation of the role of hostess.) 'As I was saying, I have no home now, alas, and so I am sadly obliged to carry my few poor little possessions with me wherever I go. Mrs. Rampage has been so kind in allowing me to bring them here,' Mrs. Roach said gently, as if she appreciated more than words can say all Mrs. Rampage's goodness to her.

Bede began questioning her politely about which articles she was claiming belonged to her.

'These . . . and this . . . and this . . . ' she said, moving about the room and touching the things pensively.

Mrs. Rampage actually shrieked aloud when Mrs. Roach came to the Persian rug.

'She's mad! *You* know that's mine, Geoffrey. Tell her you've seen it here dozens of times!'

'Luna, please!'

'Well, ask her to prove it! I can bring a dozen people to swear they recognize it. Henrietta, for one, would swear it belonged to me; she'd remember it all right.'

'Luna, I must ask you to let me handle this in my own way.'

'You're simply encouraging her,' Luna muttered reproachfully.

'Of course, when things have been in one's family for years, one would hardly hope to have the original bills to show,' Mrs. Roach pointed out mildly. 'I'm afraid the only evidence I have to offer is the fact of possession,' she said, with her three-cornered smile.

But it was when she came to the things she said Mrs. Rampage had given her that she was able to offer proof: real, valid, evidence-in-law. Because — as she said she had told Mrs. Rampage — she had made a note of each present, at the time, in her diary. (She did not explain to Mr. Bede, because he was a lawyer, and she was sure he knew as well as she did those two vital factors of British Justice: that possession is nine points of the law, and that the written testimony of a diary is accepted as evidence. These two texts were for her all the Law and the Prophets.)

She showed him the entries, turning over the pages with her finger . . . the table lamp . . . the lace mat . . . the electric kettle, so that she could make herself hot bottles or a cup of tea without going all the way downstairs (so kind) . . . the lap rug . . . the little old armchair for a Christmas present . . . the china cherub for her birthday . . .

'Lies! All lies!' muttered Luna, from the window.

'Of course, if dear Mrs. Rampage wants the things back now, she must have them,' Mrs. Roach said contemptuously. 'I shouldn't dream of keeping them. But I did just want you to see that I was speaking the truth — she did give them to me.'

'It's all made up,' insisted Mrs. Rampage, with her back to them.

'That's what she always says,' Mrs. Roach murmured confidentially. 'And it does distress me so, though I know the poor dear can't help it: she forgets. That's her trouble now, the poor old soul.' She gave him the faintest accomplice's glance, but his eyes when they met hers were quite bleak.

Mrs. Rampage rapped sharply on the window to deter Winky Woo, who was making a neat little sitting-down place in the flower bed, so she missed this murmuration.

'Anyone can write anything in a diary; that's not proof,' she said.

Mrs. Roach gave a little laugh. 'Really, dear, what does *your* word prove, if it comes to that? But I've already told you you can have them all back; if that is what you want.'

'I want my other things back too, the things you say belong to you: the rug, the looking-glass, the piece of stuff you're using for a bedcover,' Mrs. Rampage said, quite calmly and reasonably.

'But, Mrs. Rampage,' Mrs. Roach protested, 'I can't do that!' She turned to the lawyer and said plaintively, 'I can't make her believe they're mine.'

Bede went across to Mrs. Rampage.

He murmured: 'Luna, if she returns the things she says you gave her, I should let her go.'

'Let her walk off with all my other things? Geoffrey, don't be stupid! That rug alone is worth a hundred pounds at least.'

'Oh, if you want to prosecute, that is another matter. You told me you only wanted to get rid of her.'

'So I do. But I can't let her go off with hundreds of pounds' worth of stuff.' Mrs. Rampage began to cry.

Mrs. Roach stood up too, looking rather pink but very upright and courageous.

'I think I ought to tell you why I haven't left before, Mr. Bede. I haven't taken Mrs. Rampage's dismissal, because legally she cannot dismiss me. I was engaged and am paid by Mrs. Getaway, and so I presume I am only entitled to take my notice from her.'

At these words, Mrs. Rampage stopped pretending to cry, and her mouth fell open, as if a trap had snapped down on her. It brought back vividly the memory of the woman saying there had to be someone to look after her or she would be put away. She was assailed again by the terrible fear that it was true, that Cissie knew of it and this was her way of protecting her.

But it is one thing to be afraid, and another thing to acknowledge that fear. In a frantic attempt to stave off Geoffrey learning about it, she said: 'Oh, it's hopeless, Geoff! Don't waste your time any longer. She's just a pathological liar. She'll just go on offering you one lie after another as long as you care to go on listening. Don't bother! Come away!'

'One moment,' Bede said politely. 'I'd like to find out a bit more about this, if you don't mind.'

'I tell you it isn't true, Geoff. If it is, why didn't she tell me about it before? She's had plenty of opportunity.'

'Mrs. Getaway particularly did not wish her to be told; she thought Mrs. Rampage would resent it,' Mrs. Roach said to Bede.

'A somewhat anomalous position for you,' Bede said thoughtfully, touching the chair legs absently with the tip of his cane.

'It has often been very uncomfortable. I have tried to do my duty,' she said smugly, 'but if it had not been that Mrs. Getaway was so far from home and had beseeched me to look after her aunt — yes, beseeched me,' Mrs. Roach repeated, 'I should have asked to be released long ago.'

'What exactly was the arrangement between you?' Bede asked.

'You understand that Mrs. Rampage paid me no salary.'

'I kept you,' Mrs. Rampage said sharply.

Mrs. Roach gave her silvery laugh.

'Oh, my keep! I had to ask Mrs. Getaway to pay me extra for the food I had to buy myself. I think Mrs. Rampage wanted to starve me out!' She laughed again, not kindly. 'Mrs. Getaway arranged with me before I came here that I should be a sort of companion to her aunt — Mrs. Getaway knew she ought not to be living alone — and as long as I was with her, Mrs. Getaway would pay me two pounds ten a week.'

'How does she pay you?' Bede asked. 'Isn't she in South Africa?'

'Yes. She simply sends me a cheque on her English bank, and I get it cashed. Look, I haven't cashed this week's yet; I can show it to you,' she said. And she did. Producing it in quiet triumph, with the little note enclosed, in Cissie's sprawling hand.

'I don't believe it,' Luna still persisted hopelessly, as they went downstairs. 'Then what am I to do?' she wailed, when Bede assured her it was true.

'Cable your niece the facts and ask her to send a formal dismissal,' Bede advised. 'It's the only thing you can do.'

'I've already written to her all about it,' Luna said, thinking of the cost of a long explanatory cable. 'Won't that do?'

'Well, that, my dear, is entirely up to you,' said Bede. And lifted his hands to show there was nothing more he could do.

She went to the gate with him, trying to bring herself to ask the one question, as one hopelessly asks a defaulting lover,

'Do you love me?', knowing the answer in one's heart but refusing to believe it in the mind. So she strained her face up to his, and said huskily: 'You do believe me?'

In the shrill spring light she looked old; dreadful; horribly pathetic. He looked away.

'My dear girl!' he said, and patted her hand. 'If she gives you any more trouble, let me know. Dreadful person!' he said cheerfully.

Tears came into her eyes; she was absurdly grateful for his loyalty, his judgment. Only later, when she came to think it over, did she see that Geoffrey had done nothing. He had not made the woman go, he had not even frightened her into giving back the things she had taken; he had only uncovered that black traitor Cissie's beastly little plot. And how did that help her? It left her worse off than before. He was one of those men who offer to mend a piece of machinery for you; and, having taken it all apart, can do nothing with it, and so leaves it in pieces on the floor for you to deal with as best you can.

Still, he hadn't liked the woman. He had seen through her with his trained legal eye. He had seen she was a crook.

She went back into the house thoughtfully.

From her eyrie at the top of the house, Mrs. Roach could *hear* her, banging around below like an angry wasp in a glass.

Mrs. Rampage was always a noisy thinker: the harder the problem, the more racket she made. Conscious, deliberate effort of thought was alien to her, and therefore difficult to practice. It was clear enough to her that she had to get rid of the woman, and yet retain her own possessions; what made so much noise was thinking how this was to be done.

Intentionally or not, Mrs. Rampage brought matters to a head the next day by going down to the cellar to break into Mrs. Roach's trunks. She was sure some of her things must be hidden in them.

The sudden quiet bothered Mrs. Roach and she crept softly downstairs to see what the crazy old thing was up to now. At first she couldn't imagine where Mrs.

Rampage had got to, and then she heard the hammering blows from the cellar and guessed.

She opened the cellar door. Beneath her in the brightly lit cellar one trunk already lay raped, disembowelled, entrails draped over the sides and scattered in heaps on the floor. Mrs. Rampage was murderously violating another with the heavy steel poker from the drawing room.

Mrs. Roach's whole being was instantly flooded by a flush of ungovernable wrath at this wicked, blatant attack on her personal property. It was an outrage! Of course the old woman was mad, she had said so all along! How dared she, how dared she touch her private possessions!

Mrs. Roach hurled herself down the vertical steps like an avenging angel, the wings of her yellow scarf flying . . .

'Keep away!' cried Mrs. Rampage, defending herself with a scream of fright.

9

Well, that was how it happened. Almost an accident. Except that psychologists say there are no accidents, there is no involuntary action. The dropped glass, they say, expresses the conflict and indecision of the mind that let it fall. Nothing is accidental, in the sense we take it to be.

Call it *murder*, then. Yet how appallingly easy, trivial even, the dreadful finality of that act can seem in imagination. Hardly more significant than the passing of a teacup or the flicking of a switch. One thinks, There is the nagging wife, or the bedridden old man upstairs, lying so forbiddingly, so stiflingly, across the mouth of life, and beyond whom can faintly be glimpsed the exhilarating plains of freedom. The temptation is evident, the advantage apparent.

It is only later, when the act is done, that one finds those exhilarating plains fissured here and there dangerously with small cracks of fear: fear of the footsteps in the echoing street at night, fear of the eyes caught unexpectedly watching across the crowded café or cheery saloon, fear of the word or the name leaping at one innocently out of the newspaper to make the heart turn over in the breast. Fear, like an animal stirring in its den, exercising its claws, and then falling asleep lightly again.

Some there are who kill and know neither fear nor guilt, only an intoxicated surprise at themselves. They go down their familiar streets, their inward-gazing eyes wide open, and see nothing but their own savage thoughts. They are the unremarkable people with quiet impassive ways. The kind the neighbours trust. They are not disturbed by the sound of steps at night or the thought of eyes watching them; they are secure in the irrationality of their act. They are the ones who learn from a newspaper the name of their victim.

But Mrs. Rampage was not of that happy band; although to begin with she was too stunned to feel either guilty or afraid. It was just sheer physical funk that sent her scrambling out of the cellar, as she would have fled shrieking from a mouse. She clapped the door shut and turned the key.

'It was an accident,' she told herself, panting. 'It wasn't my fault. I only meant to keep her off — she looked so wild — and she got her silly head in the way. They can't say I did it!'

But *we* know the psychologists would say that Mrs. Rampage's blow could not have been so accurate or so forceful if it had not expressed the true intent of her mind. If she had only meant to frighten the woman, her aim would have wavered. *Murder begins in the mind.* For a long time the old woman had wanted to get rid of her companion; many angry hours had been solaced by the fancy of kicking her down the stairs or under a bus; and now she *had* killed her: the intention had passed into action.

No one can be the same as they were before, after killing a human being. As Mrs. Rampage was to learn. Inevitably, it alters the moral perspective. Swearing to the point of self-hypnosis that it was merely an accident cannot alter that.

To begin with she felt nothing, thought nothing. As a multicoloured disk appears to be white when it is rapidly twirled, so the rapid incoherence of Mrs. Rampage's thoughts practically made her mind a blank. She ran out into the garden with the key clenched in her fist. And then the stupidity of running away struck her. She glanced round to make sure she was not being spied on, and then, almost without knowing what she was about to do, she dropped the key down the grating over the kitchen drain.

A great feeling of relief swept over her; now not only could no one get into the cellar, but she nourished the absurd primitive notion that the enemy down there could not get out! The sun darted out approvingly from behind a dark April cloud and positively *squirted* its warm beams over her. She lifted her face to its caress in sheer animal delight: it was good to be alive!

The rain had brought out the sharp

scent of wet leaves. A few drops glistened in her hair, where she had brushed against the laurestinus bush, and trickled down her brow. The sensation froze her. She had the instant horrified conviction that it was *blood*; that she stood there like Cain, exposed to the view of any chance-may-come, with her guilt on her brow.

She stumbled back into the kitchen with her hands over her face. For her life she could not have looked in the glass! And though she washed herself scrupulously, the incident left a mark permanently on her mind. Even afterward the sight of a stain on her clothes would make her heart lurch. She was never again to feel immaculate, though she washed her hands twenty times a day — those small fat hands, writhing in soap, like two little animals tumbling and wrestling with one another.

It might have been better for her to have sent for the police right away. She honestly did consider it. Only, perhaps she considered it too long and became afraid; afraid of their questions; afraid that they would not believe her story. For, look at it how you will, it was not a very good little story: what *had* she been doing down in the cellar with a heavy steel poker? The truth was not only shameful, it hardly sounded reasonable. She could only too plainly imagine the disbelief on their bullying enigmatic faces. She could only too clearly hear their cold voices say, 'I'm afraid that is not what *we* call an accident, madam. We shall have to ask you to step along to the station with us.' And then would come the piece she had so often read, about anything you said being used against you. As for inventing any story that would cover the facts and stand up to the police's searching questions, she did not think herself clever enough for *that*. The more she tried to think of a way out, the more muddled she got.

No, it was useless, useless! In no time at all she found herself living through her trial at the Old Bailey: there was Jonquil, haggard and in tears; herself innocently condemned (for she thought herself innocent but trapped by appearances); she could even feel the cold of the prison bars biting into her cheeks as she pressed against them desperately to cry out, like Dreyfus in a film she had seen twenty years ago (it came back to her now): '*I am innocent! I am innocent!*'; but no one answered; no one came, until the Governor gravely entered to tell her that her appeal had failed —

In a cold sweat, she jerked herself out of that horrible daydream. How stupid to let her thoughts run away with her like that! She was amazed to find the kitchen quite dark already. And she looked up to see the trees outside had become black silhouettes against a sky of that peculiarly washed-out lavender which precedes the twilight. But *l'heure exquise* was just the hour Mrs. Rampage hated most.

She locked the back door. The shadows in the corner of the kitchen made her shiver, and she scuttled to the door. Her eyes were averted, but something made her turn her head; something forced her to glance over her shoulder. She stifled a shriek.

A light was burning in the cellar.

It was impossible: but it was true. Her silly old legs were like jelly. And then she gave a feeble laugh. Of course, she had left the light on herself. What a donkey, frightening herself into a fit! But the next instant she was dismayed to recollect that the light could not be extinguished now: *she had thrown away the key*. It was dreadful, but there was nothing to be done; it would just have to burn itself out. A shocking waste of money, but it couldn't be helped.

It was better upstairs, with the baize door between herself and the basement shut. She turned on all the lights to make the place look more cheerful, and soon the laughter of radio comedians was filling the house, for company.

With so much glitter streaming forth and the pleasant din of music and laughter, the neighbours might have supposed there was a party at No. 5!

She meant no disrespect to the dead. She never thought of it like that. She simply wanted to make life seem a normal business again.

'Oh, it's nice to be on one's own once more!' she said aloud, with a bright smile. But she looked very small beneath the brilliant chandeliers; she looked very much alone surrounded by all her mirrors endlessly reflecting her among all her chairs and tables. 'There's nothing to be afraid of, you stupid,' she said.

But she *was* afraid. She kept glancing over her shoulder at the doorway, as though she expected at any minute to see that tall figure coming toward her, with its hypocritically meek smile and the blood glistening like wet paint among the looped gray hair.

Mrs. Rampage was determined not to be silly. She meant to spend a busy evening working over her curios; she had not had the heart to bother with them for a long time. Now she fetched the baize cloth and spread out the brushes and powders. This was an unfailing formula for soothing her mind when it was troubled. Yet hardly had she seated herself at the table and picked up thc silver parrot swinging in its silver cage than the whole idea went stale on her, became nauseating. The room was cold, she told herself, and it was too much fag to set a match to the fire; it wasn't worth it; she was tired. 'Bed!' she declared aloud to the little silences that eddied behind her.

But when she got to her room she again changed her mind. She felt too restless to sleep. Her fat, bothered old hands, rummaging about, found an old airmail pad at the back of a drawer and it occurred to her to write to Jonquil. Yes, that was what she needed: to tell Jonquil all about it, to write down all that had happened, to confess to the only one that mattered, and be absolved.

The words poured out of her like tears, spilling across the page in an unpunctuated race.

My darling Baby [she passionately scrawled],

Something terrible has happened — Oh your poor old Mum, but it wasn't her fault — You know I told you about that dreadful dreadful woman, well she turned out even worse than that and all this time has been taking my things, the thief — Even your Uncle Geoffrey could do nothing with her, I say it is all Cissie's fault in the first place but it is too late to go into that now, it is done. Well what was I to do darling — there was no one for me to turn to and I was in despair — I couldn't repeat the things that woman said to me . . .

It was not what she wanted to say, but the thing somehow would not get itself said; she moved round and round it, expostulating, accusing. The excuses came into her mind as she wrote. (Of course she need not send the letter if she didn't want to.) Encouraged by this absurd thought, she wrote: *The woman is dead now.* But here her hand faltered, and she added *and I don't know what to do. I'm afraid*, then crossed it out. She thought a moment, and then put warningly: *They may think I did it.*

But even that was a betrayal and she hurriedly built ramparts of nonsense round it. Still, she had mentioned her predicament, indicated her danger, however vaguely; it was, she felt, up to Jonquil to read between the lines.

But that timid little phrase was no

confession and, if it had not been for an uncomfortable superstition that expressing thoughts gives them a living wayward reality of their own — because words once uttered can never be regained — she would like to have written out the truth quite baldly, in all its shocking brevity, over and over again all down the page: *The roach is dead. The roach is dead. The roach is dead. And I killed her.*

But it was too horrible even to admit to in thought, and she turned away from it desperately to write:

Dearest, I wish you were here, and underlined it with a trembling wrist; for words unemphasized were not strong enough to carry all her longing and futile hunger for this daughter of hers, who regarded with indifference the offering of her mother's foolish old heart.

Then she sealed it up and put it away in a safe place. In her innocence she thought that 'if anything happened' that would be evidence of her innocence.

She was unimaginably weary. She

kicked off her slippers, undid her corsets, and then got into bed.

She was in the kitchen with Mrs. Roach, and suddenly to her alarm she noticed that the meat loaf Mrs. Roach was nonchalantly slicing was not a meat loaf at all but her precious letter casket! She tried to cry out, but her voice made no sound, and to her horror she saw Mrs. Roach was just about to tip the sliced casket into a pot simmering on the stove. With her naked legs in their heavy boots, she somehow dragged herself across the kitchen to stop her. Mrs. Roach had already lifted the lid of the pot and she saw inside, with incredulous horror, a stew of all her most treasured pieces — ivories and porcelains bubbling hopelessly away. 'If you won't feed me, I've got to eat something,' Mrs. Roach explained, with her hateful meek smile. 'Ah, never!' she thought, and snatched up the pot, and then somehow unluckily spilled the boiling stuff over Mrs. Roach, who let out such an appalling yell, such an agonized wail, that the sound of it woke her in terror.

She lay there like a stone but for her beating heart. She was deep in the nightmare still, for the sound of the scream was ringing in her ears. 'It was only a silly dream,' she kept telling herself soothingly.

The high, inhuman shriek wailed out again. And this time she could not say it was a dream. She did *not* believe in ghosts, but a cold air wandered past her face, and it felt as though the room, or someone in it, was watching her. With an enormous effort of courage and of will she turned on the light.

There was nothing, of course. She had known there was nothing. The cold air came from the open window. She jumped out of bed to shut it. The third scream caught her at the window and froze the back of her neck; she couldn't budge. It was while she stood there trembling, staring out into the dark with wide frightened eyes, that she saw the eyes glittering at her. She thrust a knuckle between her teeth. The piercing, soulless cry rang out again. Mrs. Rampage leaned out into the night.

'Winky Woo!' she cajoled softly. 'Winky

Woo!' She clicked her fingers. 'Puss, puss, puss!'

But the cat, interrupted in its funeral oration, crossly jumped down from the wall and disappeared into the impenetrable shadows.

The next morning, with the sunshine streaming in through the open windows, she felt a different person. Gone was all her silly nervousness of the night before. She must put *all that* out of her mind, she told herself firmly.

There was a bulky envelope from Eleanor for Mrs. Roach. She took it down with her to the kitchen to read over breakfast, but the funny thing was that she simply couldn't be bothered to wade through it; the savour seemed to have gone out of the jest. Perhaps it was because she didn't want to think about *that person* any more ever. She had to open the letter because it was too thick to be torn, folded as it was. Words and phrases caught her eyes. There appeared to have been a disagreement, and Eleanor was admitting she had been in the wrong and apologizing and explaining all over again her point of view. There were eight pages. 'Well, at least she's been spared that,' Mrs. Rampage said flippantly and tore them across and across. They fluttered into the dustbin like confetti; so pretty and gay, she thought. The words, ' . . . forgive . . . reproaching . . . unhappy . . .' stared up at her from the refuse. A shadow fell across them and a voice said, 'Good morning, m'm,' making her jump (and there she was in her old wrapper with her nightcap on askew!).

'What do you want?' she said crossly.

'To read the electric meter, m'm, if you please.'

She turned rather impatiently at this interruption, and he was almost over the threshold when a sudden wave of blood through her body stopped her. She had recollected that the meter was at the head of the cellar steps.

'No, you can't,' she stammered out quickly, almost pushing him back. 'I'm sorry. I forgot. It isn't — convenient, not just now. You'll have to come some other time.'

'Ah,' he said, ruminatively, not at all put out, staring straight over her head into the dark kitchen. 'You know you've a light burning down there,' he remarked, more as an assertion than a question.

She could feel herself redden stupidly; her hands fidgeted on the door jamb.

'I know,' she said. 'The door's locked, and — and my housekeeper carelessly lost the key. I'm having another one made.'

'Ah, that's it, is it? I thought it was funny. Well, per'aps you'll be so good as to let me know when it will be convenient to call again.' And he touched his cap civilly enough, but it would be hard to say what he really thought, whether he thought it queer, or whether he didn't think about it at all.

It scared old Mrs. Rampage, anyway. She wasn't taking any chances. She kept the back door locked after that so that no snoopers could find their way in. And she kept on the watch herself most of the time at one window or another; it was easy now that she had the house to herself again to do as she liked in. She had the neighbours to consider; people were always so damned nosy about other people's affairs. It would never do for them to notice anything.

And that brought her to The Case of Winky Woo, who sat all day in the bare branches of the ash and remorselessly watched the house. That wouldn't look well after a time, someone would be sure to notice. She did her best to entice the wretch home with a saucer of milk and some pieces of fish in a bowl, but it left them untouched. Stupid creature! Alternatively, she tried to scare it away, but it merely stared down at her with baleful unblinking gaze and took no notice. 'One squeak out of you tonight and you'll get a nice bucket of cold water,' she promised. Ugly brute!

It was not long before she took against the kitchen, of course. To begin with she did not fancy to be down there after dark — a silly, childish trait, she acknowledged, but there it was — and then it came about that she disliked to venture down there even in daylight. When she did go down, it was just to snatch something out of the store-cupboard and dart up again. She couldn't stay there long enough to do any cooking, so she gave up eating hot food. She might have eaten out, once a day anyway, if she had not been afraid to leave the house unguarded. She opened tins from her store-cupboard or slipped out when night fell to buy little bags of food from flyblown cafeterias. And it seemed to her that she had solved the great Food Problem; it was so much simpler to eat out of paper bags — no more pans and plates to be washed up! No more cooking! She even fancied in a curious way that she was happy.

On the sixth day of the New Era, Henrietta rang up.

'Ducky,' she exclaimed in her exuberant way. 'What have you been up to?' She could hardly have begun more inauspiciously.

'Me? Nothing? Why?' said Luna crossly.

'Such an age since I've seen you. What's happened to you?'

'Nothing particular.'

'Oh! I thought you might have been ill, as I haven't heard.' She added affectionately: 'So I thought I'd give the old girl a blow on the blower and hear the dirt.'

'I haven't got any to tell you,' Luna said obstinately.

Well, Henrietta knew old Luna when she had a mood on her, and that it often took quite a time for her to loosen up and tell whatever there was to tell; something seemed to inhibit her, like a mental chicken bone in the throat. The best thing was to take no notice; so Henrietta began telling her about a set of Baxter prints she had bought, and a pair of luster candlesticks that she was keeping for Luna to see in case she fancied them. Only Luna must make up her mind about them soon because she had a customer interested.

And it was odd, for Luna hardly asked any questions about them; merely said that if she wasn't in in the next day or two, Etta should let them go. So unlike old Luna! Perhaps that woman of hers was getting her down.

'What about 'the roach'? What's she been up to lately?' Etta asked lightly, and was astounded to hear Luna say she was gone.

'Gone!' cried Henrietta. 'But aren't you

thrilled? My God, fancy you never telling me, you black-hearted rat! When did she go? What happened? Tell me all! I can't wait!'

'Oh, about a week ago.' (Stick to the truth where possible!)

'But how did you get rid of her in the end? I want to hear everything,' Henrietta said generously, considering how often she had been bored to tears with tales about that tiresome person.

But this time, all Luna said was: 'She just went.'

'Just like that? You don't mean it? How extraordinary! You must be frantically glad, anyway. You ought to have given me a tinkle and we could have had a little celebration; it deserves it after all this time. Where's the old thing gone to?'

'I've no idea.'

'Do you mean to say she never told you? I've never heard of anything so fantastic! Won't she expect you to forward her letters?'

'How should I know what the woman expects? If I'd known you were so passionately curious about it, I'd have asked her,' she snarled irritably.

'What's the matter, old girl? Anything wrong? You don't sound yourself somehow.'

'Thanks, I'm quite all right; just busy.'

'And bloody bad-tempered,' said Henrietta, flaring up suddenly as she was wont.

'Oh, go to hell!' said Luna, and hung up. If there was one thing she could not bear, it was interference; and if Etta didn't know that by now, it was damned well time she did.

And Henrietta, indignantly replacing the receiver, said, 'She can fly in hell before I'll ring her up again, the miserable cow!'

And that was precisely the result Mrs. Rampage hoped for. She did not want to see anyone; especially dear Etta, who had the longest nose in the world and could read her like a billboard.

10

Of course Mrs. Rampage could not exist solely on the purchases she made at the scruffy little cafés which stayed open after dark. There were other things she needed, and for them she had to rely on the telephone. Although in that district only the milk was delivered, because the old thing lived alone and said she was ill and could not get out, the shops took to delivering what she wanted. People are like that; they will always rally round and help when one is in trouble. They brought the things to the front door at her request, 'to save her going up and down stairs'; and in that way the tradesmen's entrance became obsolete and moss grew on the basement steps.

Some of the shopkeepers were obliging to the point of being tiresome. Mrs. Flinch, the greengrocer's wife, was a perfect pest with her nosiness. The good-hearted soul made a point of bringing round the order herself, and seeing if there was anything she could do for the poor old dear. She looked for a cozy gossip about Mrs. Rampage's malady, but for all her artful questions she could not get the old lady to commit herself. She tried her with various gruesome anecdotes about relatives of hers with varicose veins and kidneys and so on, but it was hard to chat convincingly through a half-open door, and the old lady would never let her get a foot inside, though she offered to do a little scrubbing or polishing to save her.

'You ought not to live alone,' Mrs. Flinch would say indignantly, 'it's not right. You need someone to look after you. Whatever happened to that nice lady you had living with you?'

Nasty, awkward, inquisitive questions! Mrs. Rampage often thought it would be simpler to go without fruit and not have to bother with the greengrocer at all.

'I'll just slip this nice cucumber in with the rest of the order for the party at No. 5. It'll do the poor old dear good.'

'Now then, Floss,' her husband would

cry from the back of the shop, 'don't you go giving away stock!'

'What d'you take me for!' she'd call cheerily back.

For there was always some little extra in the basket, a cucumber or a peach, and how could Mrs. Rampage refuse to pay for these delicacies when the damned woman made such a point of bringing the stuff round personally? It was always another shilling or two on the bill. In fact, shopping by telephone was not a bit satisfactory: one was palmed off with any old rubbish. And the costs went up. That was the annoying part of it: every bill had to be paid by cheque, which of course made the bank charges mount hideously, and then on top of that there was twopence for every cheque and a twopenny halfpenny stamp on every envelope. It sounded petty enough, but it told in the end. And although it was safe enough to slip out after dark to the postbox on the corner, or even to pad up and down the street for a breath of air, she would not venture out by day for fear of being caught by the inspector from the

Electric Light Company, or someone of that sort.

For the man kept coming round to try and read the meter, but of course she never answered the door. She let him ring and ring till he grew tired and went away. Usually he left a card in the letterbox for her to fill up and say when she would be in. Once she saw him peering in at the kitchen window with his hand over his eyes like a sailor; and it made her nervous to know that the thin yellow line was still visible round the cellar door. If he didn't think that odd, he must be an absolute idiot!

What was the use of the Electric Light Company requesting her to read the meter herself and fill up the enclosed form, when she hadn't a notion what the figures should be? She might get it hopelessly wrong if she tried to guess, and that would be worse than anything. Far better to ignore it, as she ignored everything else unpleasant.

If only people would leave her alone!

When friends came to see her, she just took no notice and pretended she was out. When they telephoned, she was rude, as she had been to Henrietta. It was self-defence more than anything else; she was afraid of their questions and their prying; it made her too nervous to bear, and she simply said, 'To hell with them!'

Once, Geoffrey rang, as a gesture, to ask if all was well or whether she required any further assistance from him; and when she assured him 'the person' had gone, he said with male smugness, 'Ah, I rather thought so!'

Another time, she was startled when she answered the telephone to hear somebody say, 'Can I speak to Mrs. Roach, please?'

'No,' she shouted out. She damned nearly let out the fatal words, 'She's dead!' But she managed to catch them on her tongue and say instead, 'No, you can't . . . she's not here. She's gone away,' she blurted in her agitation.

The agitation appeared to communicate itself to the other end of the line, and the voice stammered, 'Not . . . ? But . . . When . . . ? Could you tell me her address, then, please?'

'I can't tell you anything. She left suddenly. I don't know where,' said Mrs. Rampage, in a fluster.

'Something must have happened,' the voice said, half to itself, slowly.

'Well, you won't find her here,' snapped Mrs. Rampage, her wits sideslipping a bit.

'No, but —'

'Three minutes,' said the operator.

'Oh, please! I've no more change. Just this one question: Have you forwarded her letters?'

But there was no reply. Only a click, and silence.

Mrs. Rampage had replaced the receiver, for that was a question she did not know how to answer. She saw in a flash her blunder. All those letters of Eleanor's, for instance, she should never have destroyed. They ought to have been returned marked 'Address Not Known'. Destroying them, she had destroyed the only credible bit of evidence that the roach had left her house.

It was altogether an unnerving little episode, and it served to increase Mrs. Rampage's fear — not dislike — of the telephone. Yet she was so dependent on it, it was her one link with the outer world, so how could she do without it?

She waited uneasily for Eleanor (it had been Eleanor, hadn't it?) to take some further steps.

*   *   *

Eleanor, at her father's bedside, went over that queer fragment of conversation again and again. The old woman had sounded so odd and angry. What could have happened between her and Norah? (That Norah could have gone away without letting her know, without a word, was too painful for her even to explore at this unhappy crisis of her life, when she longed more than ever for Norah's sweet comfort, longed to run out into the world until she found her again, but instead was doomed to sit at the old man's bedside where he lay dying — at last, but perhaps too late.) 'Well, you won't find her here' struck Eleanor as a queer thing for the old woman to have said; it didn't seem to mean anything, but it bothered her and she could not get it out of her mind all the time she was wiping the old man's lips or lifting him higher on his pillows.

⋆ ⋆ ⋆

And then Peacock came back. 'God has sent him to me,' the old atheist said gleefully, for she saw at once how she could use him.

'Turned up again like a bad penny!' he greeted her, with his guilty grin.

'Where have you been all this time?' she said sternly. She wouldn't have been a bit surprised to hear he had been in prison.

'We bin ill,' he said, ducking his head like a kid.

'Didn't it occur to you that I'd have got another gardener in all this while?'

'We could clean your winders. Do anything. We don't mind what we do so long as we can turn an honest shilling,' he said, his false, evasive eyes slithering away from hers.

'There are odd jobs,' she mused. 'I've been ill too. You could do my shopping for me. The doctor doesn't want me to go out.'

They came to their little arrangements: he was to cash her cheques at the bank, pay the books, and do her shopping for her. She was trusting him, she said piously, she hoped he would not betray that trust. And if he was going to let her down, he'd better not take on the job at all, for now that she was alone she would be depending on him.

'The other one gone?' asked Peacock.

'She's been gone some time.'

As soon as he was gone, Mrs. Rampage wrote to the telephone company telling them to disconnect her as from this date, as she was going away. With Peacock to serve her, she no longer needed the telephone. It was a wonderful relief to be without it. She felt secure, inviolable as an oyster in its shell; now no one could get at her.

One of the first items she commissioned Peacock to buy for her was a roll of cheap wallpaper with which to cover up the cellar door with its betraying light. (That light always worried her.)

Papering over the door was a difficult and exhausting job, and it didn't look like much when she had finished it. If anything, it looked rather more noticeable than before with its grubby patchwork. So now to cover up the paper patch! She achieved this end by clearing all the stuff out of the dresser and moving it inch by painful inch in front of the cellar door. When the china was replaced, the door was entirely hidden. All the same she was thankful to get out of the kitchen, which, to her conscience, was full of sinister thoughts and suggestions.

She need hardly have gone to all that trouble, for barely a week later she found herself without electricity. The company had grown impatient and had cut her off.

Not that she cared! What was wrong with candles? Nobody had complained about candlelight in the eighteenth century, which was the most civilised period ever known. She liked it; she preferred it, actually: the mellow light transported her into the past, where elegant people gossiped over their game of loo. It was amusing to feel, when she wrote, like Boswell, sitting unbuttoned at his table with a goose quill in his hand, writing his journal by candlelight; or, when she read, to imagine herself to be Horace Walpole reading a letter from Mme. du Deffand. Only, one had to be very careful not to be carried away into the lives of these romantic dead or it became too sad: when one thought of poor frustrated Swift, poor Dr. Johnson with his metaphysical terrors, poor old Mme. du Deffand, blind and lonely, or poor Mme. de Sévigné — How even the best of them had suffered! How sad it all was! How they crowded in on one with their miseries! It did not bear thinking about, so painfully did it bring to mind her own situation. In particular, Mme. de Sévigné's adorable letters she dared no longer read, so exquisitely pathetic it was to see herself in Mme. de Sévigné's sufferings over her indifferent daughter.

And yet it was her fond hope that Jonquil was changing, was needing her more; so it seemed from her last letter — which Mrs. Rampage carried about in her spectacle case so that she could read it a hundred times a day, reading fresh meanings into it each time. The folded shred of paper was as precious as a kiss. Her daughter wrote with a certain anxiety to know if she was well, as it was so long since she had a letter from her mother, but to Mrs. Rampage those words were vibrant with tenderness. After all, it was only natural that as she grew older and more understanding (so Mrs. Rampage had always hoped and prayed) she would turn more to her mother.

She thought: 'Perhaps Jonquil is going to have a baby and that is her way of telling me. She's so shy and modest, she would expect me to read between the lines. In that case, I should go out to her at once. Yes, there is no reason why I shouldn't simply shut up the house and go out there for a visit; that would be best for all concerned.'

From that time she began to comfort herself with elaborate plans for going out to Malaya. She did not mention any of this in her letters — it was to be a great surprise! — lest Jonquil should forbid her to come. As for the letters, it is true she wrote them, but somehow they never got posted: she forgot, or she was afraid they would worry Jonquil. At all events, they accumulated at the back of her desk among the bills without her properly realizing it. Anyway, the letters didn't matter if she was going out there. She resolutely refused to admit that she would never dare to go out there without her daughter's permission.

Time passed in these idle speculations and she did nothing. It was lucky May was warm, for she subsisted more and more on any odds and ends of food at any hour that she happened to feel hunger; she never had anything hot to eat now that the electricity was cut off, not even a cup of tea unless she boiled a kettle on the fire — but that was a bother, and she got into the habit of drinking raw milk. ('So good for the nerves,' she declared. For it was always her way to cheer herself up over things that other people preferred to grumble about.)

* * *

People in Edenbridge were quite shocked that the very day after the old man's funeral, Eleanor Fielding went up to town; it looked so unfeeling somehow. Not that Eleanor cared what they thought. She had only one idea in her head. To find Norah.

Her idea was to go to No. 5 and try to get some sense out of Mrs. Rampage. At least find out what had happened between them; why Norah had walked out like that, when her very last words to her had been that she couldn't leave Mrs. Rampage; couldn't and wouldn't, and didn't want to. Hadn't that been the core of their bitter quarrel (Eleanor had been such a jealous fool, she admitted it now ruefully enough)? So what had made Norah change her mind so suddenly? She might learn that from Mrs. Rampage even if she could not give her Norah's address.

She *saw* the old woman — that was the extraordinary part of it! — she could not have been mistaken, it plainly was the old woman, though she looked half-crazy with her hair wild round her staring face. Eleanor saw her at the window as she came up the path. She was only there a moment, but Eleanor could not have imagined the figure. And yet, though Eleanor rang and rang, and hammered on the door with the knocker, no one came to answer. She could not make it out. Unless the old woman had gone suddenly deaf. But even that wasn't a solution, because the old woman had seen her as plainly as she had been seen by Eleanor; she could tell that by the momentary look of fright that had passed over the old creature's face as their eyes met.

Eleanor squinted through the letterbox but there was nothing to be seen. She bawled through the aperture like an urchin: 'Mrs. Rampage! Mrs. Rampage! I know you're there, I saw you.' (Mrs. Rampage heard her and made a face, though her knees shook.)

At length, defeated, Eleanor gave up. She was heavy-hearted, at a loss how to trace Norah now. She would not know where to begin, her only clue having failed. She felt despairingly that all was over forever, that Norah did not want to be found by her. Perhaps it was her cruel way of dismissing Eleanor. For surely no one could let her anger burn for so long against a person she loved?

When she reached the gate, she looked back once at the house, in the hope of catching another glimpse of Mrs. Rampage at one of the windows. But there was no sign of her.

There was something else, though, like a sign from heaven! On the parapet of the roof sat Norah's little cat, Winky Woo, like a patient ghost. She could not think what it meant, Winky Woo being there. It was so extremely unlike Norah to have parted with her. She did not know what to think. But she could not go on standing there like a fool, with her mouth open and her eyes popping out of her head. Abruptly, she opened the gate and disappeared.

★　★　★

Eleanor's visit gave Mrs. Rampage a great fright. And the worst of it was that she came back again the very next day. And the day after. Mrs. Rampage saw her walking around the house, trying the windows. The impertinence of the woman! It was persecution! Suppose next time she broke a pane and forced her way in, what on earth should Mrs. Rampage do?

It was horrible! There was no one to whom she could turn for help now. The poor old thing was in a perpetual tremble, her heart racketing about boisterously like a sheet in the wind. She could not bear to be spied on like this; as if the woman knew something.

Soon Mrs. Rampage was living in her house as within fortifications: the shutters locked over the windows and heavy pieces of furniture barricading the doors. It was the only way she could feel safe, in the womb-like secrecy of the dark. She shuffled about interminably with her candle seeing that all was secure.

' . . . An old woman alone . . . One hears such dreadful tales these days . . . Anybody might learn of the valuable things I keep here. That Mrs. Flinch, always asking about my stuff. Now *she* was a talker . . . ' In such muttering phrases did Mrs. Rampage rationalise to herself her extraordinary way of life. They were impossible conditions of existence, but she had made the terms herself.

Henrietta Purvis had been ill with gallstones. She had been a month in a nursing home, and then a fortnight's convalescence at dear old Brighton, and after that there was so much to attend to when she got home that it was another week before she had a moment in which to ring Luna and find out why she was still sulking. Henrietta could not understand why Luna should no longer be on the telephone. It was so extraordinary that it worried her, and at the first possible moment she went round to No. 5 to find out.

It gave her quite a turn to find the place all shut up, as though Luna were dead or something. She wasn't strong enough yet to stand shocks; it brought her out in a sweat.

Luna was the sort of person who *never* went away from home. Nothing would induce her to go away. Short of Jonquil breaking her neck, of course.

Yes, that must be it. Something must have happened to Jonquil, and she had flown out there without stopping to tell anyone what she proposed to do. In too much of a flap, no doubt.

On her way home, Henrietta stopped at the post office and bought a sixpenny airletter on which to write a teasing letter to Luna in Malaya. Wouldn't she be surprised to hear from her!

11

A couple of days after this, by one of those coincidences so oddly frequent in life, Henrietta received a letter from Malaya. But not from Luna. It was from Jonquil, agitated and indignant:

What can have happened to Mother? So unlike her not to write. It's weeks since I've heard. I write and write and get no answer. Is she ill? I haven't fussed unduly till now because I always supposed you would let me know if there was anything wrong.

'That's it, put it all on me,' snorted Henrietta.

My dear Jonquil
I'm afraid I have no idea where your mother is. I thought she was with you. Unfortunately I have been rather ill for some weeks and during that time have

neither seen nor had word from your mother. It was only this week that I was well enough to go round and see her, only to find No. 5 closed up — a house of the dead! She has evidently gone away somewhere. She may even be on her way out to pay you a visit, perhaps feeling it was useless to wait for an invitation, and you know how she longs to see you [wrote Henrietta, coolly hitting below the belt].

It might have occurred to her to be uneasy over Luna if it had not been for Jonquil's letter, which annoyed her. As it was, she was thunderstruck to receive a cable five days later instructing her to inform the police immediately. What on earth was the matter with Jonquil? Did she imagine that something had happened to Luna? What could have happened? Though indeed, she thought with an involuntary shudder, anything might happen nowadays to a woman living alone, and an old woman at that. So she pinned on her red straw hat and went round to the Culloden Road Police

Station at once to report that the old lady from No. 5 had disappeared.

'No. 5!' said the sergeant, looking faintly surprised. And then he drew a paper toward him and said gruffly, 'How long ago?' (It often saved a lot of time to ask this question before one filled in the other particulars, because often enough the missing person would be only a few hours overdue.)

'I don't know. It may be as long as a couple of months,' Henrietta was obliged to confess. 'I've been away ill, myself. When I went round to see her I found the place closed.'

'Hmm,' said the sergeant, writing. 'Relative of the missing person?'

'No, I'm only a friend.' She thought he gave her a curious look, and she hurried on to explain about Jonquil's cable.

'Hmm. Now we'll have a few particulars, if you please. Name of the missing person?'

'Luna Adeline Rampage.'

'Rampage?' exclaimed the sergeant, jerking up from his task.

'Yes. Have you heard anything of her?'

But policemen are like doctors: the questions they don't wish to answer they ignore.

As soon as he had pumped out of Henrietta all she had to tell, he sent her away, telling her that he would let her know as soon as there was any news.

He went through to the inner office.

'Some more information about No. 5 just come in, sir.'

'Oh? What?'

'Brought in by 'a friend' again, you see, sir,' he said, laying the sheet before the inspector. 'Same complaint: missing in suspicious circumstances.'

'But this is about the other woman!'

'Yes, sir. Interesting, isn't it?'

Their eyes met.

'What did you say?' asked the inspector.

'Told her she'd hear from us as soon as we had any information to give.'

'All right.'

'The Fielding woman is a proper crank,' the sergeant said conversationally. 'She's taken up her abode at No. 17, so's she can watch what is going on. Doesn't think the police are up to it, lot of lazy slackers,' the sergeant added sardonically; but the inspector was busy writing and did not raise his head.

It was true about Eleanor Fielding; she was disgusted with the indolence and incompetence of the police. She had gone round to them in terror and they had practically laughed at her fears. They maintained it was possible and even probable that Mrs. Roach had left her cat temporarily at No. 5 because she had nowhere to take it.

'You think I'm an hysterical old maid,' said Eleanor, 'but I know there is something wrong. Something has happened to her, to my friend, and I'm sure the old woman knows about it. Or else why wouldn't she let me in? I do beg you to search the place.'

'I'm afraid we can't do that, miss; not without a warrant, and we haven't sufficient grounds to apply for a warrant, you see,' the sergeant said reasonably.

The more uncalled for, then, for Eleanor to say tartly, 'Do you have to wait for a murder, then, before you can get a warrant?'

'Hardly, miss. But we must have evidence enough to convince the coroner that a search is necessary.'

'I dare say if you searched the house you'd soon find evidence enough,' she said, with a bitter laugh.

'You'd stand more chance of doing that, I dare say, than we would — if you could persuade the owner to let you in.'

'She won't do that; I've told you. I don't know why you don't think that suspicious. I thought the police were always on the lookout for that sort of thing. I thought that was what we paid our taxes for — to prevent crime, or at least uncover it.'

'There's no law that I know of, miss, against a person choosing to shut theirselves up in their own homes if they've a fancy to. This is a free country, you know.'

'Free for whom?' said Eleanor, stalking out.

The police were not quite as idle as Eleanor supposed in her wrath. They did function; they at least performed their compulsory devoirs; and it was a duty to examine conscientiously every piece of information laid. Obviously, these matters had to be dealt with discreetly; if everyone knew what they were about, they would get nowhere very fast. The police weren't fools — at least, not such fools as that!

These routine inquiries took time as well. The same man couldn't be used for different types of work. It was the plain-clothes Sergeant Charles who tackled the neighbours (after tackling No. 5 and failing to be admitted). Suspicious, irritable housewives melted before his dark-eyed persuasive charm. His smile as he said, 'I haven't come to sell you anything,' was both playful and reassuring.

He told the young married woman from the ground floor of No. 3 that he was making a house-to-house survey for a BBC Listener Research questionnaire.

'It's rather rot, isn't it?' he said cheerfully. 'Most people seem to switch it on in the morning and leave it on all day regardless; they haven't a notion what they're hearing.'

'Like the woman next door,' she said, casting up her hands with a grimace.

'Oh, is she one of those? I tried there just now, but there was no one at home. Well, I needn't bother with her, then.'

'She was at home all right.'

'I didn't hear the radio!' He laughed.

'Oh, she doesn't always — as a matter of fact, I haven't heard it going for some time,' she added slowly. 'I hadn't realized it till just this minute. How funny! Perhaps the poor old thing's ill.' She looked thoughtful and rather pretty, considering with reluctance her duty.

'Does she live alone?' the nice sympathetic man asked.

'I believe she does now. She used to have rather a nice companion-person till a few weeks ago. I knew her slightly because we went to the same church.' Her eyes went to its distant spire as she spoke. 'But, between you and me, I think she found the old lady rather difficult.'

'So she upped and left,' he suggested idly.

'Maybe,' shrugged the young woman. 'Or maybe she got the push. I wouldn't know.'

'She didn't confide in you to that extent.'

'We weren't *friends*,' the young woman said rather haughtily, feeling that this conversation had gone on long enough. 'I simply noticed that she wasn't in church anymore. And even then I didn't think anything of it for some time, because her cat was still around. But it was always hanging round our back door, mewing, and finally I realized she'd left the poor little thing to starve.'

'I thought you said she was a nice person? I don't call that a very nice way to behave. I bet you feed it,' said Sergeant Charles.

'Well, we do, as a matter of fact; but it won't come in.'

'Ah, I thought so,' he said gaily. 'I'm a great judge of character.' And he moved on to other matters.

The elderly servant who lived opposite at No. 4 was more communicative. She led such a lonely life looking after the grumpy, deaf, old entomologist she worked for that an opportunity for gossip was not to be lost. It came gabbling out in a furtive stream. Nodding at him knowingly, arms akimbo, she might have been back in her own village street in Wales wagging her tongue to a crony.

Ah, she had noticed . . . Yes, and she had thought it queer . . . Never had she been one for gossip, but facts were facts, weren't they?

The point was, whether Mrs. Roach had gone or whether she was still at No. 5, she had not been seen again by any of the neighbours; nor had anyone seen her leave (as she had been seen to arrive — in a cab with all her trunks!).

The vicar of St. Anne's said guiltily, 'Oh, dear, I'm afraid I've been very remiss! I did venture there once to inquire if she had been taken ill — she was such a splendidly faithful supporter, you know, that I quite miss her attendances — yes, yes, but there was no one at home. So I took it that the dear lady was away. I should of course have tried again. Most remiss,' he said hollowly, shaking his head. 'I trust nothing is wrong, however,' he added after a moment, with a faint gleam in his eye.

'Why should anything be wrong?'

'My good sir,' said the vicar, with the asperity of one who has been taken for a fool, 'you would hardly be paying me this call otherwise. You are from the police, I opine?'

However, the vicar was not entirely useless. He was able to confirm more nearly than anyone else the date of Mrs. Roach's disappearance. Mrs. Roach had been a daily communicant. The last occasion he had administered the Sacrament to her had been the Wednesday after Easter.

That was two days after she was last seen by Miss Fielding.

It was at this point that the second witness had entered the scene in the person of Henrietta Purvis. Undoubtedly, someone was still living at No. 5 since the milk was taken in daily; but which of the two women it was was not yet clear to the police. It was queer, though, that each woman should think her friend had disappeared.

PC Wright was given the dull perseverant inquiries from shop to shop. Mr. Bull, the butcher, said that Mrs. Rampage hadn't taken her rations for close on two months. Todtale, the grocer, said that he had been delivering goods to No. 5 for a period when the old lady was ill, but now she sent a man round to fetch what she wanted. The bank manager said that he understood Mrs. Rampage was ill. She sent someone round to cash a cheque every Monday. Yes, perfectly in order; signature unmistakable.

Sergeant Maxwell was instructed to go round and ask Mrs. Purvis certain questions. For instance, did she happen to know the name of Mrs. Rampage's solicitor? Oddly enough, she did; it was not a name you could forget — the Venerable Bede. There were other questions too, which Henrietta answered with increasing impatience.

'Meanwhile,' she burst out at last, 'what has become of my friend?'

'Oh, she's there, madam, at No. 5.'

'In that shut-up house?' screamed Henrietta.

'So it would appear.'

'Are you crazy?'

'We have reliable information to that effect, madam.'

'I don't believe it. You don't know Luna. The gayest . . . Someone must be keeping her there against her will. I never did trust that woman; she'd a mouth like a trap.'

'Who is that, if you please?'

'A creature who called herself Mrs. Roach. Came as a sort of companion, and then my poor Luna couldn't get rid of her. Poor darling, she nearly drove her mad . . . ' But even as she said this, she recollected that the last words from Luna had been to assure her that the woman had gone, and all her fantasies of Luna murdered or kept prisoner in her own home subsided like a house of cards. 'Then you mean . . . But what can have happened to her to make her live like this?'

'People do sometimes go funny and shut themselves away. You'd be surprised, madam, how often we come across it.'

'It's too dreadful! Can't anything be done?'

'That would be up to her family.

There's nothing the police may do. It's not against the law to become a recluse if that's your fancy. But if her family like to take steps . . . '

So Henrietta cabled to Jonquil:

MOTHER SERIOUSLY ILL
ADVISE YOU TO COME OVER
IMMEDIATELY.

Inspector Hunt represented to Mr. Bede that inquiries were being made about the disappearance of a Mrs. Norah Roach, lately a companion of his client, Mrs. Rampage.

Bede regarded his fingernails superciliously. 'We know that she left our client's on or about the eighteenth of April. We were in communication with our client on that date and she definitely informed us that the person had left.'

'How did the subject arise, may I ask? Did you mention it or did she?'

Bede allowed his alter ego to drop out of the conversation.

'I did.'

'There had been some trouble in that

quarter?' hazarded the inspector.

'A little difficulty,' he conceded. 'My client had come to me for advice in the matter . . . I'm not sure that this should go any further.'

Inspector Hunt said gravely that it was of the highest importance.

'The woman *was* a thief, then?' said Bede. 'Well, my client had no wish to charge; she would prefer to keep out of any public scandal, I know. The difficulty in her case was to get the woman to *go*: a certain complication of contract.'

'Ah?' said the inspector phlegmatically — as if he neither understood nor cared. 'Now, what would that be?'

'A rather unusual situation,' mused Bede, 'though there was a similar case in Judson v. Barker and Cruikshank, 1907.' He explained Mrs. Getaway's well-meant but mischievous arrangement, whereby she engaged Mrs. Roach and paid her, while allowing Mrs. Rampage to believe she was her legal employer. In law, there was nothing Mrs. Rampage could do.

'If she was really a thief . . . ' began the inspector.

'That was a little hard to prove. Her contention was that my client had given the chattels to her; the items were mentioned as gifts in her diary.' Bede glanced across to see whether the inspector grasped the cunning of this. 'However, you now have evidence, I take it, of other felonies.'

'To revert for a moment, if you don't mind, to the other matter, the woman Roach's so-called engagement by the niece on behalf of Mrs. Rampage. How did you know that was not a further story she had invented to prevent her dismissal?'

'I saw the cheques,' Bede said simply. 'Mrs. Getaway sent her weekly cheques on her English bank, from South Africa, where she is at present residing, it appears.'

'It may be interesting to check on that, if you can give me Mrs. Getaway's bankers.'

'Yes; I got that point too,' Bede said approvingly. 'It was The Westminster, Baker Street branch.'

It was no great matter to check up at the bank how many weeks had elapsed since Mrs. Roach had last cashed a cheque from Mrs. Getaway: it was nearly eleven.

Clearly, then, no cheque had been cashed since her disappearance; she had not needed to use them for money.

The following Monday, the police nabbed Peacock when he came into Lloyds Bank in the High Street to cash Mrs. Rampage's weekly cheque.

'We just want to ask you a few questions down at the station,' said PC Wright in his ear, catching him by the elbow.

He went as yellow as a quince.

'I'm not taking it,' he said. 'Ask *her*! I get it from *her*.'

'That's all right,' they assured him cheerfully, and marched him off, looking very small between them, his head turning anxiously from one to the other.

It took a little while to calm him down, to make him understand that he wasn't being accused. At first, he was too on the defensive to answer the questions properly, but presently he got the hang of it.

No, he never went inside the house. To begin with, she used to come outside to give him his instructions. After that, she used to open the front door on the chain.

Now she passed the list and the money to him through the letterbox, and he pushed the things back to her the same way.

'How does she know when to expect you?'

'I knock,' he said, 'like this,' and he rapped a tattoo on the desk.

'What do you see when you look through the letterbox?'

'Nothing to see,' he shrugged. 'It's pitch in there. Beats me how she finds her way about!'

'She doesn't put the light on?'

'Not so far as I ever seen.'

'What does she use for illumination, then? For lighting,' the sergeant added.

'I buy candles. Three or four dozen a week.'

'Do you, now?' mused the sergeant.

That was how they came to approach the Electric Light Company, from whom they learned that Mrs. Rampage was a 'bad debt' and her supply had been cut off in consequence. The meter inspector had called many times; they had written three times besides, without result; and finally they had been obliged to switch off supply, the Company not being a charitable concern.

The meter inspector gloomily remembered the incidents of his various visits to No. 5. (Fruitless calls were the most depressing part of his depressing job. His feet gave him hell!) So he remembered all right going there that April day, and the lady being just about to let him in when she suddenly changed her mind and decided it wasn't convenient. No. 5, he informed the gentlemen of the police, being an old-fashioned sort of house, had its meter down in the cellar. It was always the habit in the 1900s to fix the meters in the darkest, most un-get-at-able spot in the whole house!

She told him the cellar door was locked, and her housekeeper had lost or anyhow mislaid the key. She was having a new one made, she said.

'Of course, it wasn't for me to call the lady a liar,' he sniffed, in his sour, unbeatable way. 'I just said, very cool, 'You know you got a light burning down there?' She knew what I meant all right,' he said, with a superior smile.

'How did you know a light was burning in the cellar?'

'I could see it,' he said, a shade indignantly: suspicious people cannot endure suspicion in others.

'Through the cellar door?' inquired the policeman.

'Now, look 'ere — '

'I'm asking you.'

'It's pretty darkish down there, being a basement; from where I stood in the entry I could see across the room the light shining round the door. Morehover,' he said haughtily, 'hon other occasions when I called, I noticed the light showed round the door. You'll always find that it's them as don't mean to pay as is the most reckless with the current. Shocking wasteful, some people! Lights burning all over the house, just to save theirselves the trouble of switching them on and off, I dare say,' he grumbled. 'The party at No. 5 was like that.'

12

Jonquil arrived in London from the airport soon after nine, and went straight to Henrietta's. Henrietta was sweeping the shop prior to opening it, with her head tied up in a duster. It was hardly an hour for callers.

'Hallo, Etta,' said Jonquil, as the little blue front door opened.

'Jonquil!'

'Well, don't look so surprised. Didn't you expect me?'

'Why on earth didn't you let me know you were coming, my dear?'

'You sent for me. And I came as quickly as I could manage.'

'Well, thank God you have, I say!'

'Aren't you going to ask me in? I've come rather a long way.'

'*My dear!* Look at me goggling on the doorstep!'

'How is Mother?' Jonquil asked, as soon as she was inside.

'I don't exactly know,' said Henrietta evasively. 'Have you had breakfast?'

'I had some coffee at the airport; I'm all right. What do you mean, Etta, you don't know how she is? What's the matter with her?'

'Let me get you something to eat then, my dear girl.'

'I don't want anything.'

'A cup of tea at least,' insisted Henrietta, lighting the gas with a plop.

'Etta, please answer my question. What is the matter with Mother?'

'I'd answer it if I could. I don't know, Jonny. I haven't seen her.'

'I don't understand,' said Jonquil sharply. 'Where is she?'

'In her home, we presume. Do sit down, dear, and try and relax: tea will be ready in a minute.'

Jonquil had had a tiring and anxious journey, and now to have to cope with Henrietta's prevarication made her want to scream. God, old people were impossible!

'I really don't want any tea. I wish you would explain, Henrietta. You cable me that Mother is seriously ill, and I go to considerable expense and trouble to get leave from my work and fly over, and when I get here — '

'Keep calm, keep calm, my dear girl! These things can't be blurted out all at once, *you* should know that.' Henrietta dipped a spoon into the teapot and stirred vigorously. 'The fact is that the poor old darling has gone a bit funny and she's shut herself up in that damned great house of hers, the way people do sometimes, and simply won't see anyone or let anyone in. It's got to be stopped; she can't go on like that, can she? But the police say it's up to her relatives, no one else can do anything. It's not illegal to become a batty hermit, apparently. Sugar?' she said, handing Jonquil the cup. 'Well, I did think of Rhoda, naturally, as being the nearest; but then I thought, well, what's the use, they never did get on. No, obviously the only person she'd listen to is you. I couldn't explain the situation in a cable; I simply did what I thought was best.'

'All right,' the girl said wearily. 'Thank

you, Aunt Etta. I'll go round at once.'

'Shall I come with you?'

'I think it will be easier to tackle alone, thanks all the same.'

Mrs. Rampage had bought No. 5 after Jonquil's departure for Malaya, expecting her daughter to return within the year, but she had married out there, and her mother had been left with this big, useless house on her hands. Seeing it now, desolate, a forlorn garden with a few weedy, unpruned roses fading beside the path, Jonquil could not imagine why her mother had been so captivated by it; it struck her as dreadfully dingy. It was hard to believe that anyone still lived in this deserted place.

She did try ringing and knocking of course, but without much hope of success, and the windows were far too securely fastened for her to be able to force an entry. Eventually she scribbled on a scrap of paper: *Let me in, Mother; I've come back to see you. Jonquil*, and pushed it through the letterbox. She could hear someone shuffling about somewhere inside, and at last she called through the aperture of the letterbox: 'Mother, it's me! Do open the door, for goodness' sake!'

Mrs. Rampage heard the voice with a start of pure terror, disbelieving her ears.

'Who's there?' she said loudly. 'What is it?'

'It's me! Jonquil!' the girl called crossly.

'Jonquil's in Malaya.'

'Well, I've come home.' The absurdity of bawling such an idiotic conversation through a chink in a door, like Bottom and Flute! 'For God's sake, do buck up and open the door, Mum! I've been here half an hour already.'

'All right, my darling; I'm coming, I'm coming,' said the old woman in a trembling voice, trying to undo the fastenings with her shaking hands. 'Jonquil! My darling! My pet!' she sobbed, falling into her arms. She touched her daughter with little tentative pats like a blind person. 'Why didn't you tell me you were coming, dearest?' she cried, laughing with joy through her tears.

'There, there, Mother! It's all right. It was all decided in such a hurry that I hadn't time to let you know. I thought I'd give you a surprise.'

'Let me look at you! You're lovelier than ever, darling. Does he adore you? Are you wildly happy?'

Same old Mum, probing away into one's personal life. But she didn't look the same old Mum; she was horribly changed — gone to seed. Jonquil almost didn't recognise her. She was the flabby waxen white of one who never knows daylight and good fresh air.

'But we mustn't stand here, my darling,' Mrs. Rampage said quickly, suddenly noticing her daughter's stare. She slammed the door and bolted it again, then picked up her candlestick and led the way into the drawing room.

'Why the darkness, Mother?'

Mrs. Rampage tittered uneasily.

'Darling, it's so wonderful to have you here! I can't believe it.'

'But why are we in the dark?' Jonquil persisted.

'Darling, I'm afraid your naughty Mum overslept this morning. I've only just come down.'

'Well, it's terribly stuffy in here. Let's open up and have a little air.'

'Well . . . Oh dear . . . ' murmured Mrs. Rampage, uneasy, but not daring to protest.

'How do these catches unfasten? It's so pitch dark in here, I can't see. Do switch on the light, Mum.'

'Look, I'll show you. It's quite easy,' her mother said quickly, turning the iron buttons that secured the bars. The strong, unaccustomed light made her blink till her eyes watered.

She sneezed and rubbed her nose on the back of her hand. Jonquil noticed the black-rimmed nails, the stained and ragged wrap, and the hair hanging in matted curls on her neck; she looked unwashed, uncared for, and bloated. These signs of degeneracy, the watering eyes and sneezing, made Jonquil wonder whether her mother was taking drugs — that would account for everything. It would account, too, for the lies she told when Jonquil pressed her with awkward questions.

Breathing in pure air again turned Mrs.

Rampage giddy. She clutched at a chair back and would have fallen if Jonquil had not caught her and thrust her head between her knees.

'Sit still! I'll go and fetch you some water. Where's the kitchen?'

'No! No!' cried Mrs. Rampage, starting up in a panic. 'I'm all right. It was the shock . . . the excitement of seeing you . . . Stay with me, darling, stay with me!'

'Have you had breakfast?'

'Yes, yes,' she murmured, catching her child's hand and pressing her lips to it.

'When did you have it? You told me you'd only just woken up.'

'I had it just before you came, my darling. How perfectly splendid you look with your hair like that!'

'In the dark?' said Jonquil.

'What, dearest?'

'I said, did you eat your breakfast in the pitch dark?'

'Oh, darling, don't you bother about me.'

'I do bother about you. I bother about you a great deal.'

Mrs. Rampage's heart swelled with joy

at these cross words, the words she'd waited so long to hear.

'Do you, darling?' she said fondly. 'It's worth everything to me to hear you say that. Oh, how I've missed you!'

'Then why did you never write?'

'I did write, dearest. Of course I wrote. But it's all been such a muddle. But now that you're here, it will be all right; I feel it.'

'I haven't had a letter from you for months, Mother. I've written and written to ask you what was the matter, and you've just never answered.'

'I can't believe that, darling; it wouldn't be like me not to answer your dear letters that have always meant so much to me. Sometimes they've been the only things that have kept me going. You'll think me very weak, but you're young, darling, and don't know; sometimes the loneliness and despair . . . ' Her voice cracked and faded.

'Despair?' cried Jonquil sharply.

'Oh, not really, of course,' said Mrs. Rampage quickly.

'But if you read my letters — '

'Read them!' exclaimed Mrs. Rampage, fumbling in the pocket of her wrap and producing two tattered and grubby airletters. 'Just look how I've read them! I carry them about with me everywhere.'

'Then you must have seen how worried I was at never hearing from you, and I can't understand why, if you're as fond of me as you pretend, you never answered me.'

'You can't have got my letters, darling.'

'That's exactly what I'm saying,' said Jonquil irritably.

'Yes, the post has been most unreliable here lately. I believe they steal them. It must be a great temptation for the postmen. But I bless them for it,' she said, her face gladdening, 'because it's brought you back to me.'

'What dreadful nonsense you do talk, Mother.'

'I love you to scold me. You're sweet.'

Jonquil drew her beautiful mouth into a narrow red line. She must not lose her temper just because it was her mother. She must treat her as she would one of her patients. She must passionlessly drive her mother to face the truth. Unluckily, it was not only now in her illness that she lied; she had always been evasive and untruthful.

'One letter might get mislaid, not half a dozen,' Jonquil said firmly, watching her.

Mrs. Rampage looked away.

'Wait!' she said, scuffing off in her dirty old mules — with the uppers splitting away from their soles, Jonquil noticed, and a fat white toe poking out through the side. She was back in a moment. 'You don't believe me? Look!' she said, and poured the letters into Jonquil's lap.

Jonquil stared down at them. *Mrs. G Bracebridge . . . Mrs. G. Bracebridge . . . Mrs. G. Bracebridge . . .* in her mother's wild writing. The words appeared to waver.

'What's this?' she said more gently.

'The letters I wrote you, dearest.'

'Why did you never send them, dear?' she said, with only a hint of impatience in her tone.

Mrs. Rampage put a hand to her head.

'I was ill,' she said. 'I've been ill. I didn't want you to know.'

'What was the matter with you?'

'My head,' she said, tears blurting from her eyes.

'But, my dear Mother, of course you feel ill and get pains in the head if you live in a mausoleum; you might as well be buried alive. It's ghastly! The place is positively foetid; it smells like a slum,' Jonquil said sternly, wrinkling her nose in disgust.

Mrs. Rampage gave a nervous, appeasing giggle.

'Yes, it's all very well, Mother, but you ought to have more sense. I thought you had someone to look after you. What's become of that nice woman you told me about?'

'She's gone,' said Mrs. Rampage carelessly, and added quickly: 'But, Jonquil, you haven't told me a word yet about yourself. There's so much I'm dying to hear.'

But Jonquil, determined to keep her to the point, said severely, 'Wasn't it rather foolish of you to get rid of her like that?' and was astounded to see her mother change colour.

'I — I — ' stammered Mrs. Rampage,

taking this as an accusation, taking the words 'get rid of her' in their pejorative sense; she was badly frightened, less at Jonquil's discovery — it hardly surprised her that Jonquil should be omniscient — than from dread of her wrath.

Jonquil watched the fat little fingers plucking restlessly at the edges of her gown.

'I — I'd rather not talk about it,' she brought out.

'Why not? You said she was so nice, so kind. What went wrong?'

'She wasn't. She was a dreadful person.' She shuddered and put her face in her hands. 'Ask anyone. Ask Geoffrey. Ask Henrietta, she couldn't *bear* her. I was perfectly wretched with her. No one could blame me.' She just peeped through her fingers to see Jonquil's expression. She was frowning like a vexed Italian angel. 'Don't be angry with me. Please! Try to forgive me, my darling,' she murmured in a choking voice.

'Really, Mother dear!' Jonquil sighed with exasperation. 'Do try not to be so emotional, it's so bad for you. You shouldn't be dependent on my approval or disapproval, it's not healthy.'

'I know, dearest,' said her mother, surreptitiously wiping away the tears. 'I will try not to be so silly. You know I only want to please you.'

Jonquil spread out her fingers hopelessly. What was the use of talking?

'Hadn't you better go and get dressed, Mum?' she suggested wearily.

While her mother was upstairs dressing, Jonquil wandered from room to room unfastening the shutters and opening the windows. The place was stagnant, dust everywhere, and cobwebs netting the corners. There were even some greyish-brown flowers drooping in a vase, so long dead that it was no longer possible to identify them. It was like exploring a tomb. Could Mother have been here all this time? she wondered. Would she ever have let the silver tarnish and the glass film over? Her lovely creamy ivories were already brown with neglect, the porcelains powdered with dust. What had happened in that short time? Or was it not so short a time? Had it been approaching all the years of her absence?

The kitchen might have had no one in it for weeks. She was surprised to find nothing in the larder except a shelf of tinned food. Not so much as a slice of bread! What had her mother been living on all this while? There was a mystery here, and the sooner she uncovered it the better. She went upstairs.

'Mother, I'm hungry. I've had no breakfast.'

'My poor angel! What a thoughtless pig of a mother you've got,' she said, running around in her knickers. 'I'll get you something at once.'

'Don't bother. I'll get it myself if you tell me where to find it.'

Mrs. Rampage stooped down by the bed and produced a half-full bottle of milk and a paper bag with some stale cake in it.

'If only I'd known you were coming, I'd have got something in,' she said apologetically, 'but living alone, I don't bother much about food.'

'Do you ever have a proper meal, Mother?'

'Darling, at my age one needs very little.'

'Can't be bothered to cook, eh? You've

got yourself in a thoroughly bad state. We'll have to change all that now, won't we?' Jonquil said in her brisk, persuasive, professional voice. 'And we'll begin by taking you out for a really decent meal, so put on your best bib and tucker.'

'Oh, darling, I really . . . I don't . . . ' she said, flustered.

'Nonsense! It's all part of this silly fad of behaving like a recluse. It's got to stop. It's not normal to lock yourself up and live in the dark.'

'I'm not mad, if that's what you think,' the old woman muttered.

'Of course you're not. But people will say you are, if you behave so oddly.'

'There is a reason. I didn't want you to — I thought it might worry you — but now I shall tell you. I had a very bad burglary here not long ago. It frightened me; living on my own like this, anything could happen. So I thought it best to keep the place locked up.'

'Did you tell the police?'

'The police are no use. You don't know what England's like nowadays, Jonny.'

Jonquil of course wanted to know what

had been taken, if she'd got compensation from the insurance company, and how long ago it had all happened.

'In any case,' she said, 'I don't suppose they'll burgle the place while we're out for half an hour.' She meant it for a jest, but her mother took it quite seriously.

'But that's just what they will do, darling,' Mrs. Rampage protested. 'You don't realize what a lot of valuable stuff I've got here, worth thousands of pounds. It's well known; they have men posted about to watch for me to leave the house.'

'My dear good Mother, what on earth is the use of having all these possessions if you have become such a slave to them that you never dare put your nose outside the door? It's simply a mania!'

'Darling, you mustn't be angry with your silly old mum,' she begged, when a thundering knock like doom itself seemed to shake the very walls. 'What's that?' she cried, her hand to her heart.

'I'll go and see,' said Jonquil, running down.

'Don't let anyone in!' Mrs. Rampage shouted.

It was the police.

They were almost more astonished to have the door opened to them than Jonquil was to see them there. They asked to see Mrs. Rampage.

'She's engaged. I'm her daughter. Can I do anything for you?'

'I'm afraid not. It's a personal matter. We'll wait, if you don't mind.'

'I'll go and tell her you're here.'

When she had gone, the two men looked at one another; without speaking they carefully scanned the room, noting all that was to be seen, while they waited. They had quite a time to wait because Mrs. Rampage fought against going down to see them; she wanted Jonquil to tell them she was ill. This Jonquil refused to do, seeing no reason for it. They appeared to Mrs. Rampage as bucolic as trees, standing bare-headed in her drawing room, as if they were planted there. As always, fear made her angry.

She said, in a high scolding voice: 'What is it? What do you want? This is a very inconvenient time for you to come. Here is my daughter just arrived from

Malaya, I haven't seen her for nearly five years, and she's not been in the house half an hour when you come and pester me. It's very inconsiderate. Can't you come back some other time?'

'We shall try not to keep you long, madam. Just a few questions.'

'Some other time,' she said, straightening tables and chairs fussily, as if it was of the utmost importance to get them into some imperceptibly 'right' position.

'Ask them to sit down, Mother,' Jonquil said.

'What, dear? Oh, Jonquil darling, why don't you take your things upstairs and unpack them.'

'Would you rather I wasn't here?'

'No, of course not. But — I'm afraid you'll find it very boring.'

'All right, Mother. I understand,' the young woman said tolerantly.

'Now, Mrs. Rampage,' said the inspector, as Jonquil shut the door. 'We're making inquiries about a Mrs. Norah Roach, and we think you may be able to assist us.'

'Why?'

284

'Because we understand she resided with you for approximately six months.'

'I meant, why are you making inquiries about her? What's she done?'

'Disappeared,' said the inspector laconically.

'Really? Well, I don't think I'll be able to tell you much. She left here a long time ago.'

'When, exactly?'

'I'm afraid I don't remember the date.'

'April, was it?'

'Yes, I believe it was.'

'Well, never mind just now. Did she tell you where she was going?'

Mrs. Rampage put her hand to her head.

'Some address in the Cromwell Road. I've got it written down somewhere, I know. I dare say I could find it for you.'

'I see,' said the inspector, taken aback. 'And that was where you forwarded her letters?'

'Any that came,' conceded Mrs. Rampage.

'You are sure of that? Because it seems there are several cheques that were sent to her that have never been cashed.'

'I wouldn't know about that.' Mrs. Rampage shrugged.

'From your niece in South Africa, I understand, by whom Mrs. Roach was employed to work here as your companion.'

'That's what *she* said,' Mrs. Rampage said scornfully, alternately tugging her woollen sleeves down over her wrists and pushing them up her arms. 'All I know is that out of the goodness of my heart, and to oblige Cissie, I took her in when she was in trouble.'

'And it didn't work,' said the inspector sympathetically.

'She was an impossible person, that's all.'

The inspector nodded.

'You had a bit of trouble with her. There were words, eh?'

Jonquil quietly opened the door and saw her mother looking sulky.

'Not finished yet?'

'Nearly, miss.'

Mrs. Rampage said: 'I finally did lose my temper, and I told her to get out.'

'And she went?'

'Yes.'

'Just like that?' said the inspector. 'Without her luggage?'

'Of course not. I don't know what you mean,' said Mrs. Rampage.

'It appears that no one saw her leave,' said the inspector, with a very straight look at her. Mrs. Rampage tried to look bold and innocent, as if she didn't know what he was talking about. 'If she had taken her luggage, she would have needed a cab; and a cab would have been noticed by someone,' he went on. 'Therefore we must presume that she left here without her things — taking only a suitcase, perhaps.'

'Yes. That's what she did. She asked me to mind her things till she got settled ... and her cat,' added Mrs. Rampage. 'She asked me to keep her cat too.'

'What is all this?' asked Jonquil, frowning.

'Just a few inquiries, miss, about a missing person; one Mrs. Roach, who was residing latterly at this address.'

'I don't understand — '

'It's all right, darling.'

'Just a minute, Mother. I don't see why these gentlemen are here. If the woman is missing since she left here, what is the use of questioning Mother about it?'

'Quite, miss. We fully recognize the point. It's just a matter of a routine check,' the inspector said soothingly.

'Well, have you finished? Because we want to go out.'

'We'd just like to glance round, with your permission.'

'What for?' Jonquil asked haughtily. ('There's my brave girl!' thought Mrs. Rampage.)

'Just part of the routine, miss.'

'I don't see that it's necessary.'

'No, miss,' sighed the inspector. 'But it's orders.' He gave a fatuous laugh. 'Ours not to reason why, ours but to do and die.'

'Oh, well, let's get it over with,' Jonquil said ungraciously. 'Mother, you'd better take them.'

Mrs. Rampage tried to moisten her dry lips, tried to smile. But courage came back to her as she took them over the house; they gave but the most cursory glances everywhere, bored, like estate agents looking round new premises. The tour was conducted in silence and afterward they politely left; and Mrs. Rampage and her daughter thereupon went out to luncheon. Mrs. Rampage no longer protested against leaving the house; there was no point in it now.

'Well?' said the inspector, as they walked away.

'Yes, sir.'

'All very pat and circumspect, eh?'

'There's no knowing, is there?'

'It doesn't seem very likely, on the face of it. And yet I've got a sort of itch . . . '

'Like a hunch, sir?'

'Nothing as positive as a hunch. It's just an itch to go back and have another look. Did you notice anything in the kitchen?'

'Where the dresser had been moved, sir, and left a lighter patch on the wall?'

'Yes. That might be interesting, don't you think? Why was the dresser moved? Unless it was to hide the door to the cellar that the meter-reader chap told us about — the cellar the old girl was so anxious to keep him out of. It's just an idea,' said the inspector modestly, 'but I think it'll bear looking into.'

★　★　★

There was still a great deal that Jonquil wished to know; there were still a great many things she did not understand. It was terrible for Mrs. Rampage to have to face all these questions: and Jonquil was so persistent, so difficult to lie to. What reasonable reason could she give, for instance, that there was no electricity? To say the lights were fused would only make matters worse, for then Jonquil would certainly want to mend them; and the fuse box, of course, was in the cellar. To take her mind off these tiresome questions, Mrs. Rampage began to chatter of other things. Jonquil listened with impatient patience.

'But, Mother,' she interrupted restlessly, 'if you had become so nervous of being alone that you had to wall yourself up, why have the phone disconnected so that you really were cut off from the world outside?'

'It seemed a needless expense,' said Mrs. Rampage hurriedly.

'And then, when Etta came, why didn't you — ?'

'Oh, darling! Talking of Etta reminds me. I almost forgot. I've got something wonderful for you; you'll go mad when you see it. I couldn't send it out to you, it's too fragile to pack and far too precious. It's really a museum piece. I'll go and get her now — I call her the White Lady.' Making Jonquil a present of her treasure was a sudden inspiration which she hoped would distract the child from these awkward topics.

'Wait, Mother! Not just now!'

'Yes, I shan't be a moment, darling,' she said, scurrying out of the room. She ran up to her room, and then, to give herself a breather, took off her outdoor clothes and kicked off her painful shoes. She slipped into the dirty old mules again, patted her hair thoughtfully, and then picked up the White Lady under its glass bell and carried it carefully from the room.

She was slowly descending the stairs

with it (slowly, because the White Lady was not affixed to its ebony base, and slithered gently against the glass bell with every movement), when she heard sounds below. She paused to listen to Wagnerian footsteps mounting the stairs.

'*Who's that?*' she called in a panic. And then, '*Jonquil!*'

Jonquil came out into the hall at the same moment that the inspector appeared at the top of the cellar stairs.

Mrs. Rampage heard Jonquil say sharply, 'What are you doing here?'

From where she stood on the turn of the stairs the old woman saw the policeman hold up his hand with a yellow scarf in it — the yellow scarf! She uttered a choked cry.

They heard her and glanced up. Indeed, the last picture her mind registered was of Jonquil looking silly with her mouth agape.

Whether her foot slipped, whether her broken mule betrayed her, whether she tried to turn back on that awkward corner of the stairs in an attempt at flight, no one now can possibly tell. All one can say is that she might have saved herself; that anyone else would have caught at the balustrade. But not Mrs. Rampage. Her only concern was to save the precious White Lady, the museum piece that she fancied was worth hundreds of pounds. She would have died rather than it should be damaged. And in fact, she did.

But it was all for nothing. Though they could hardly loosen her grip on the ebony stand, later, the glass bell was shattered, and the White Lady lay at the foot of the stairs with a broken neck — like Mrs. Rampage.

We do hope that you have enjoyed reading this large print book.

Did you know that all of our titles are available for purchase?

We publish a wide range of high quality large print books including:

Romances, Mysteries, Classics
General Fiction
Non Fiction and Westerns

Special interest titles available in large print are:

The Little Oxford Dictionary
Music Book, Song Book
Hymn Book, Service Book

Also available from us courtesy of Oxford University Press:

Young Readers' Dictionary
(large print edition)
Young Readers' Thesaurus
(large print edition)

For further information or a free brochure, please contact us at:

Ulverscroft Large Print Books Ltd.,
The Green, Bradgate Road, Anstey,
Leicester, LE7 7FU, England.
Tel: (00 44) **0116 236 4325**
Fax: (00 44) **0116 234 0205**

VICTIMS OF EVIL

Victor Rousseau

A gang led by the mysterious Doctor Omega is targeting prominent New York financiers for blackmail. One victim arranges a police trap for the criminals — which fails. Revenge is swift and brutal. The defiant financier is assaulted by an unseen hand in a peculiar and gruesome manner, left unconscious and bleeding from his left eye. When he wakes, the full horror of the attack becomes apparent. For the man is still alive, but left babbling gibberish and unable to communicate . . .

THE TWELVE APOSTLES

Gerald Verner

Under the light of a full moon, amid the sinister ruins of an ancient abbey, a man gasps out his last breath as he lies in a pool of his own blood. Who, amongst the residents of the sleepy little village, has a motive for the murder? And how is it connected to twelve silver statues of the apostles, missing for centuries, and the enigmatic Abbot's Key mentioned in a criminal's dying words? Superintendent Budd is called in to solve one of his most baffling cases.

THE LIBRARY DETECTIVE

James Holding

Hal Johnson is a retired cop who works for his city's public library, tracking down missing and overdue books. But his switch of careers is no sinecure, for his work always seems to lead him into some sort of mystery, such as blackmail, robbery, kidnapping — and even murder. In the course of collecting fines and recovering books, Hal finds himself in plenty of dangerous situations that require him to use all his former police skills . . .

WITNESS TO MURDER

Norman Firth

Through her window, June Merrill idly watches her neighbour in the adjoining flats — only to see her being suddenly, savagely killed. Having watched murder being committed, June knows that she, as the only witness, is now in mortal danger . . . In *Message from a Stranger*, Mike Carr watches a beautiful woman across a restaurant. Just before she leaves with two strange men, she scrawls a cryptic note in lipstick on the table-cloth — which Mike must decipher to save her from danger . . .